WONDER HORSE BOOK TWO

I0658038

LA DUQUESA

AN ARABIAN HORSE NOVEL

THE SECOND IN A SERIES ABOUT ARABIAN
HORSES AND THOSE WHO LOVE THEM

VICTORIA HARDESTY
AND NANCY PEREZ

Authors of Action, Adventure and Suspense with Arabian Horses

PUBLICATION
CONSULTANTS
We Believe In The Power Of Authors

PO Box 221974 Anchorage, Alaska 99522-1974
books@publicationconsultants.com—www.publicationconsultants.com

ISBN 978-1-59433-785-7
ebook ISBN 978-1-59433-786-4
Library of Congress Catalog Card Number: 2018938101

Manufactured in the United States of America.

ACKNOWLEDGEMENTS

As we said in our first book, no writer writes in a vacuum. We write about our own experiences and those of others. Many of the horses in our stories are a compilation of horses we've actually known and loved. Mighty Max, for example, is "Spot" to his Mom and he really does shake the Richter Scale at 5.5 when he enters a show ring. We've seen and loved horses who "dance" and horses that "float" and horses that would jog along the rail with a perfect headset for a hundred miles if their owner asked them to.

We want to thank our friends and family for their continued support as we write our stories. We couldn't do it without the help and support of Rebecca Gordon and Sharon Zarogoza, our beta readers and editors. We also couldn't make this happen without the support of husbands Michael and Ray.

Dedication

This book is dedicated to all those young ladies who've ever wanted a horse of their own and were willing to work hard just to be able to ride one.

CHAPTER ONE

Mike Hartley and Ginny, his wife of 34 years, sat down to breakfast Sunday morning early. Mike already made the rounds of their seventy acre ranch checking to be sure all horses, cows, dogs and cats were standing upright on four legs as his crew fed, watered and mucked stalls. He generally walked the ranch each morning but this day he took one of the electric carts so he'd be done quicker. He wanted to do something special this day.

Ginny had only been home a couple of weeks. She spent several weeks at a friend's ranch in San Juan Capistrano while Walter and Caroline Howard stayed with their daughter, Becky, who was in a coma in Mission Hospital. Ginny and her friend, Sharon O'Neal, stayed at the Howard's place and took care of their herd of Arabian Horses. Once Becky was out of the woods and on her way to recovery, Ginny came home. Since then she played catch up on the things only she did at the ranch. Mike wanted to spend some quiet time alone with her.

"What would you say to going for a ride with me today?" he asked her after taking a sip of his coffee. "Just you and me.

I have a couple of horses in training that need to put some trail miles on and you need a break."

"We haven't done that in a long time," Ginny answered. "That sounds wonderful to me."

Brody, their 14- year- old nephew, shuffled into the kitchen for a bowl of cereal in time to hear the conversation. "Yeah, Aunt Gin, you two need to get out of here. Uncle Mike, you don't have any clients on your schedule until two o'clock this afternoon. Mr. Garcia is coming to see his horse. If you're not back, I can handle that for you."

"Then it's a done deal!" Mike grinned at Ginny. "Go get your boots on and I'll start tacking up the horses. Meet you in the barn."

A short while later the two were mounted and headed out the front gate. Mike suggested they take the horses south of the ranch into the hills. Clyde, their seven year old Labrador retriever, wandered along beside them, occasionally checking out interesting smells along the way. They relaxed and talked about many things. They climbed in elevation toward the peaks of the San Gabriel Mountains as they went along.

A quarter of a mile before they reached the last low hill on their route the hair along Clyde's spine stood erect. He heard something they didn't and it bothered him. He walked a little faster out in front of them. Just before reaching the summit of the hill, Clyde froze, hackles raised, and his tail stopped wagging. He crouched sniffing the air.

"What's bothering Clyde?" Ginny asked. Then they heard what sounded like a horse screaming and thrashing somewhere beyond the rise. They also heard cursing and a sound like a cracking whip. Clyde crouched low, growling deep in his throat. The whip cracked again and Clyde launched himself up the road. His big paws threw dirt and gravel behind him as he flew over the rise.

Mike and Ginny looked at each other in surprise. "That's not like Clyde at all!" Mike muttered. "We'd better go see what he's up to."

They both cued their horses from a slow walk into a canter. Gravel and dust sprayed behind the horses hooves. At the top of the rise, they halted.

"Do you see anything?" Ginny asked.

"Sounds like its coming from the left and not too far. I hate horse abuse. Let's go check this out!" Mike said grimly, his relaxed smile gone.

Ahead of them, Clyde's low growl changed to furious barking. Whoever he was barking at began cursing loudly. The whip cracked again and again.

Mike and Ginny picked their way around a rocky outcropping covered with low Juniper trees and scrub. Out in the open again, they were looking down into a small valley they'd never seen before. A narrow dirt track just wide enough for a vehicle led to a tiny cabin. Alongside the cabin was a pipe corral with a two sided shelter. The scene was shocking. The ground inside the corral appeared to be at least a foot deep in mud. The horse inside was throwing itself into the corral panels to escape. The man was cracking the whip to keep Clyde away from him. The normally mild-mannered, hundred-pound black dog continued charging the man barking furiously. The man cursing Clyde appeared intoxicated. All around the cabin the ground was littered with broken whiskey bottles, beer cans and trash. The man didn't notice the riders at first.

"Clyde! Come!" shouted Mike. Clyde turned and saw Mike and Ginny. He reluctantly walked back and sat down beside Mike's horse. A deep growl resonated in his throat as he stared at the hateful man.

Mike thought before speaking. He and his wife were probably on private property and they were out in the middle of nowhere. The man looked intoxicated and obviously violent. He didn't want to escalate the situation.

"Hey! You having trouble with that horse?" Mike asked the man when he got close enough to be heard. Ginny was right beside him glaring at the man.

"It's none of your business!" the man shouted. "You're on private property. Turn around and go."

"Well, I just thought I could give you a hand if you're having trouble with the horse. I'm a pretty good horse trainer," Mike smiled stiffly.

Ginny stared at the horse. It was a mare. She could tell it was an Arabian. But the rest she could see broke her heart. Somewhere under all that mud was a pretty face. The horse looked nearly dead of starvation. Her backbone protruded. Her hipbones and shoulder bones looked sharp enough to tear the skin. Every rib was exposed along her sides. She was covered in mud and feces. Whip welts showed on her neck, chest, sides, back and hips. Ginny couldn't tell what color she was. During the exchange with Mike, the man stood holding the whip low. The horse was standing in mud above her pasterns shaking like a leaf in a hurricane.

"You know, I've got a soft spot for those Arabian horses," Ginny began. "Why don't you let us buy her? You get cash money and you don't have to bother feeding her anymore." Ginny just happened to have five hundred dollars cash in her pocket. She planned a trip to the feed store for supplies later that day and had forgotten to leave the money at home before their ride.

The man's ears perked up at the mention of cash. "How much?"

"Well, looks like we're going to have to put quite a bit into her to turn her around, so how about two hundred fifty? Or, if you have papers on her, we can make that five hundred."

"I got papers. Five hundred sounds good. Get your money and you got a horse!" The man dropped his whip into the mud and stalked off toward the porch on the front of the cabin.

"I got it right here and now," Ginny told him. She handed her reins to Mike and dismounted her horse. She pulled a wad of cash from her jeans pocket as she strode toward the cabin porch. Standing in front of the man, she pulled bills out and counted them into his hand.

"Wait a sec," he told her and walked into the cabin. He returned a few minutes later with registration papers. He handed them to Ginny. "She's your problem now!" he turned on his heel, walked back inside the cabin and slammed the front door.

Ginny tucked the papers in her hip pocket and walked back to Mike and the two horses. "I almost forgot I had the feed money in my pocket." She smiled at him. "Can you pony my horse back to the ranch and come back here with the truck and trailer? I really don't want to leave her alone with him again. I'd rather stay and try to get a halter on her and see if I can't calm her down before we try to load her. I'll keep Clyde with me, just in case."

"You are such an old softy!" Mike said. "I'm not sure about leaving you alone with him though. He was handy with that whip!"

"I was standing a few feet from him when I paid him. I thought I was going to get drunk on his fumes. I don't think you have to worry about me being alone with him. I'm pretty sure he's already sleeping it off in there. Besides, I'll keep Clyde with me for protection," Ginny smiled up at him while she stooped and scratched Clyde behind his ears.

"Okay. I'll grab one of the guys to help us in case we need it. See you in a few minutes," Mike said as he turned and led Ginny's horse back to the road and disappeared over the top of the rise.

Ginny walked back to the corral careful not to step on broken glass. She looked around behind the cabin and found a halter with a lead rope attached laying in the muck. She also found a hose and cleaned them off as well as she could. She walked over to the corral and leaned on the top rail watching the mare. Clyde stayed right beside her.

The horse was still trembling but not as bad as before. She turned her head to look at Ginny a couple of times, looking away quickly as though she was ready to bolt at the slightest movement.

Ginny began to talk to her in low soothing tones. The more she talked, the less the horse trembled. Clyde whined softy. The horse seemed more and more curious about Ginny and the dog and less and less afraid of them. Finally Ginny rolled up the legs of her jeans, opened the gate to the corral and took a step inside. She sank into the muck. The horse flinched at the sound of the gate opening but stood still. Ginny walked toward the horse slowly while she continued talking to her. The horse stopped trembling by the time Ginny got close enough to touch her shoulder. Ginny talked and scratched her withers gently through the mud. Ginny was able to slip her halter on and get it buckled.

"Now for the hard part," Ginny told the horse. "We have to get us both out of this crud and onto dry land. So let's take this one step at a time, okay?" Ginny took the shortest route to the gate, directly through the middle of the corral. As she stepped into the goo near the middle, her foot sank deep enough for the muck to slop over her boot tops and down into her boots. She plowed on, struggling like the mare in the sucking mud. Ginny succeeded in getting the horse outside her corral just as Mike and his helper arrived with the truck and trailer. Mike opened the back door of the trailer while Ginny walked the mare toward it, being careful of the broken glass. Clyde stayed right by her side. Neither

Mike nor Ginny knew what to expect from the horse when she saw the horse trailer. They were amazed when the horse spied a bag of fresh hay and walked in as if she'd been hauled in that trailer every day. Mike followed the horse inside and tied her lead rope to the tie ring, hopped back outside and closed the door.

"Well, that was sure easy!" Mike said. "Guess we didn't need the extra help after all."

"Well, I sure need some," Ginny said as she sat on the trailer fender. "These boots are goner's and my socks too. Help me pull them off, will you? I don't want this all over the inside of the truck."

Mike grabbed her boots and pulled them off, tossing them in the truck bed. Then he picked his wife up and set her on the truck seat so she wouldn't get broken glass in her bare feet. Mike's helper climbed into the back seat with Clyde.

Ginny looked straight through the windshield holding back tears. "Let's get out of here," she said to Mike. He started the truck and drove back to the ranch, dropping Ginny off at the house to get some boots. Then he pulled the trailer in front of the main barn.

Brody met him at the truck and helped Mike unload the mare. He'd prepared a stall for her when Mike left to pick her up. "She's sure a mess, Uncle Mike," Brody said when he got a good look at her. "She needs some groceries, doesn't she?"

"Yeah, and that's probably not all she needs," Uncle Mike told him. Brody already knew the story about how they found the horse. Mike told him when he picked up the trailer. "My guess is we'll need to get Doc Martin out here in the morning to look her over and give us advice on how to take care of her and bring her back."

Aunt Ginny walked through the barn toward them with Clyde at her heels. "How was she at unloading?"

"Same as she was at loading," Uncle Mike told her. "I'd say she's been hauled a few times before. She's good on the lead too. Someone's done some work with her, just can't figure out how she ended up where she was when we found her."

Ginny pulled her registration papers out of her back pocket and opened them up. "Wow! She's a daughter of Spanish Lace. I remember her showing maybe ten years ago. She was a lovely deep chestnut with four white stockings, a pretty blaze and almost platinum blonde mane and tail. What a looker. This mare is La Duquesa. She is only four years old herself. She would have sold for a pretty penny with her breeding alone. I'd like to know how that old drunk got his hands on her and why he abused and starved her. Sometimes I wish these guys could talk and tell us their story, but then again, sometimes I'd rather not know."

"What do you want me to feed her Aunt Ginny," Brody asked.

"Looking at her, she's missed a few too many meals. Let's get her started on a bucket of soaked pellets and beet pulp with about a half a can of bran mixed in. We need to make several small meals for her for a while. We'll talk with Doc Martin in the morning about it. Don't give her any hay until we talk with him."

Brody walked off to get a bucket ready for the mare while Mike and Ginny stood looking at her. La Duquesa was standing at the back of the stall with her head in the corner. She was trembling again but not as bad as before. She looked like she was waiting for the other shoe to drop.

Brody brought back her bucket mixed and ready and showed it to Aunt Ginny before dumping it in the feeder. He closed the feeder door and stood in the middle of the barn aisle beside his aunt and uncle watching the mare. She didn't move. She showed no interest in the feed at all.

"Let's give her some privacy, guys," Aunt Ginny finally said as she walked to the barn entrance. "Maybe we need to give her some time."

Everyone but Clyde left the barn heading for the house. Clyde remained sitting in the middle of the barn aisle looking at the horse. When all was quiet, he stood. *"You know you are safe here, don't you?"*

"Are you sure? I thought I was safe before and I wasn't after all," the mare whispered.

"Tell me about it," Clyde answered.

"I remember being with my mommy on a beautiful ranch with trees and grass. There were lots of mares and babies and I had friends to play with. One day a couple showed up with a horse trailer. I was shoved inside without my mommy and driven for a long time until we finally stopped. The couple pulled me out of the trailer. I was so scared and couldn't see my mommy," the mare broke down. It took her a minute to regain her composure. *"I always felt safe with my mommy."*

"What happened then?" Clyde whined softly.

"The people weren't very nice to me. They pulled and shoved me until they got me into a paddock next to one filled with goats. They left food and water for me and left me there all alone. I missed my mommy so much."

"I didn't mean to make you sad. Please have something to eat. You will not be sad here. These people are wonderful and very kind to all the animals. Aunt Ginny especially loves her horses. We'll talk more later. Please eat. You need it to get better." Clyde begged her, wagging his tail.

La Duquesa slowly turned and walked to the feeder and began eating. As soon as Clyde was sure she would eat all that was in her feeder, he left the barn and went to join Brody.

CHAPTER TWO

Sara Evans leaned back on the sofa in her Aunt's, now her home, in Redlands, California with a hot cup of tea thinking about the past couple of months. Aunt Annie passed away of pancreatic cancer two and a half months ago. That left Sara alone in the world. Annie had been her last living relative. Sara quit her job to care for her. At Annie's request, they moved into her small cabin in Pinon Hills and constructed a corral for Annie's horse, La Duquesa. Annie loved that mare dearly. Annie wanted Quesa to be the first thing she saw in the mornings and the last thing she saw at night. Quesa and Sara were both with Annie when she took her last breath. A silent tear slipped slowly down Sara's cheek as she remembered.

Anne Stone was organized. She planned everything before she died, including her own funeral. Sara just had to follow instructions. Pictures of that time fluttered through her mind like a colorful slideshow. Some of the memories were comforting. The eulogies given Aunt Annie by her professor colleagues and many of her students helped Sara realize Anne Stone was special to more than just herself. Anne Stone was loved by so many people.

Sara remembered being in the attorney's office for the reading of the will. There was only herself, Reilly Stone and Anne's attorney in the room. Reilly was Anne's husband. He apparently expected a windfall. When the attorney finished the reading and Reilly realized he'd been completely cut out of Anne's will, he was furious and stormed out of the office leaving Sara sitting there in complete shock. Anne Stone had bequeathed her entire, sizeable fortune to Sara.

It wasn't until later, when Sara found an old box of photographs in the back of Aunt Annie's closet, that she realized Anne Stone had been in love with Reilly at one time. The photos were of a happy young couple sharing birthdays, anniversaries, holidays, and family gatherings with Anne's family. That all stopped suddenly and Reilly became absent. Sara knew he showed up infrequently, stayed a night or a couple of days and then disappeared again for months or years at a time. Anne never divorced him. He was hateful when he showed up and refused to tell her where he'd been or what he'd been up to. Over the years Anne received a couple of phone calls from women looking for Reilly. They hung up when she identified herself as Reilly's wife. She knew what he'd been up to.

Sara stared into the fireplace. Her glance fell on the framed photograph of La Duquesa hanging above the fireplace next to the framed ribbons from her National Championships last year. The gold trophies stood on the mantle under the photo. She realized she hadn't talked with Tania, La Duquesa's trainer, since the day Aunt Annie passed away. She called her that day and asked her to pick Quesa up at the cabin. Sara knew she would be too busy in the next few weeks to care for her properly. She'd seen Tania at the funeral but there had been so many people there she didn't have a chance to talk to her. She checked her watch. It was still early. She looked up Tania's number and called her.

"How's our Quesa doing?" Sara asked when Tania picked up the phone.

"I have no idea," Tania replied. "I thought you knew that."

"What? What are you talking about?" Sara suddenly panicked.

"I showed up at the cabin like you asked," Tania explained. "Some old drunk came charging out at me, threatening me. I told him I was there to pick up the horse. He told me he was Anne's husband and the horse belonged to him now so I could get off his property immediately or he'd call the sheriff and have me thrown off. He was scary! I turned around and left right away. I thought you knew."

"Oh. No!" Sara almost whispered. "Aunt Annie left me the horse and the cabin in her will, along with everything else. Reilly doesn't own anything. And he just walks off and disappears all the time. Poor Quesa. I've gotta go. I'll call you later." Sara slammed down the phone.

She ran to the kitchen for her purse and keys and ran into the garage, hitting the garage door opener as she passed. She climbed into the car but it took her three tries to get the key in the ignition she was shaking so badly. She stopped and took a few deep breaths. She had to calm down. She forced herself to back slowly out of the garage, shutting the door once she was in the driveway. She took another deep breath and backed onto the street. She drove to the freeway still shaking a little. She had visions of arriving at the cabin and finding Quesa dead in her stall. She knew there wasn't enough feed left there for her since her Aunt died. Tears streamed down her face as she begged Aunt Annie for forgiveness in neglecting her prized horse. She had no sense of time passing as she drove until she turned off on the narrow dirt road leading to the cabin. Once she crested the rise and started down the road to the cabin, her headlights lit up the area. The cabin was dark. The headlights picked up small shiny objects on the ground around the cabin. The corral appeared empty. With her heart in her throat, she parked her car leaving her purse on the seat, the keys in the ignition and the headlights on. She walked to the corral first, calling "Quesa, are you there?" She got no reply, no welcome nicker, nothing. She walked all around the corral. She didn't see the dead body of a horse. There was nothing in the corral but mud. La Duquesa was gone!

Sara climbed the porch steps and found the cabin door unlocked. She walked in and flicked on the lights. Inside, the cabin was a complete wreck. When Sara left the day Aunt Annie died, the cabin was spotless, everything in its place, floors swept and mopped, beds made. She was confronted by trash, whiskey bottles, beer cans, dirty dishes, and muddy floors everywhere she looked. She was furious! How could he? He had no right!

Another set of headlights appeared over the rise, shining in through the open doorway. Sara didn't notice as she stood taking in the mess confronting her. She didn't hear the other car door slam or her Uncle climbing the steps to the cabin until he walked in behind her and screamed, "What are you doing here?"

Sara turned on her heel and screamed back, "What are YOU doing here? This cabin is MINE, not yours. You have NO rights here! And what have you done with MY horse?"

Reilly Stone glared at Sara's red, blotchy face for a minute. "I SOLD her! If I can't have her, neither can YOU!"

"Take your garbage and get out of my house or I'll call the Sheriff and have them throw you out!" Sara screamed at him.

That was the last straw for Reilly. He charged her and slapped her across the face. Then he grabbed her around the neck with both of his large hands and began to squeeze. Sara kicked at him and swung at him trying to punch him in the face. Reilly squeezed harder. Suddenly Sara was afraid for her life. Reilly was going to strangle her to death! Her arms and hands looked for anything she could grab while she tried to knee him in the groin. He shifted his body so she couldn't hurt him and kept squeezing her neck. Just when things started going black in front of her eyes, her hand found the handle of the cast iron skillet on the stove beside the front door. With super human effort fueled by fear and panic, she picked the heavy skillet up and swung it at his head with all her remaining strength. It connected. His grip around her neck loosened enough for her to pull away. She scrambled around his large frame and ran out the front door, straight down the steps two at a time. She jumped in her car, twisted the key in the ignition and threw it in reverse. She stepped on the gas spinning her tires. Dirt flew in the air obscuring her vision as she backed away from the cabin. She turned the car and stepped on the accelerator again spinning her tires and blowing clouds of dust and gravel behind her as she drove up the road.

Sara didn't see her uncle staggering from the blow. He nearly fell out the front door backwards. He kept his feet under himself for two more steps before he collapsed. His body fell down the steps, head down and feet up. His neck hit the bottom step at just the right spot. It snapped and his head fell over at an unnatural angle from his body. He would never get up again.

CHAPTER THREE

Seven Months earlier...

Maryann Wilcox loved school. She was an excellent student and got along with her classmates. She tended toward shyness but loved the process of learning. She became an avid reader when she discovered books about horses. She'd already read every book in the school library that even mentioned horses, was rapidly going through the public library's collection and pestered her mother often enough for magazines at the supermarket and books at the local book exchange. Her reading expanded her vocabulary and improved her spelling greatly.

A few weeks into the new term, her English teacher handed out an assignment to Maryann's eighth grade class. "All of us dream about something special we would like to have or happen in our life. I want you to write a three page, single spaced, essay that tells me what you dream about." The teacher gave her students three weeks to turn in the assignment. "This will be a large part of your grade for this semester, so pay attention to spelling, grammar, and the punctuation we've been learning in this class."

Maryann's heart soared. This was going to be easy. There was only one topic for her. Ever since she could remember she had the very same dream. It was comforting to her. She dreamed about the Duchess, a silvery white mare she rode bareback across a meadow in the moonlight. She loved that horse and the horse loved her. Her 'Duchess' dreams were very special to her.

Maryann also had an artistic talent that surprised her mother and her Aunt Adele and Uncle Roy. She could fill in shapes in a coloring book without crossing the lines from the time she was a little over two-years-old. By the time she was four she was drawing horses for fun. Some of her sketches were quite good. Her mother, Rose, framed a couple and hung them up in her bedroom for wall art. They went along with the horse theme of the room. She had horses on her window curtains, horses on her bedspread, Breyer horses on her dresser and shelves of them above her bed, not to mention all the books and magazines with horses on the covers.

Maryann spent most of a week working on the essay to get it just right. She scratched out words, inserted new words, shuffled sentences around. When she was satisfied, she copied the whole thing neatly then dragged out her sketch pad and pencils and drew a picture of the scene in her dreams. When she was satisfied she had a reasonable likeness of herself and the Duchess on paper, she attached the sketch to her paper and turned it in.

The paper sat on her teacher's desk until all the students had submitted theirs. Her teacher took them home to review and grade over a weekend. She fully expected 13 and 14 years olds to write about MTV stars if they were girls, sports if they were boys, etc. She was stunned when she got to Maryann's work and saw the sketch attached. Her teacher was well aware of Maryann's situation. Her mother,

Rose, worked for barely above minimum wages at Andrews Hardware Store in Phelan, where she and her daughter lived with her elderly Aunt and Uncle. Roy and Adele were scraping by on Social Security pensions. Maryann had about as much chance at owning a horse as she did flying over the rainbow. The fact that the essay was letter perfect and from the heart surprised her and tugged at her own heart strings. The drawing topped everything.

Maryann's teacher brought the graded essays back to school on Monday. She pulled Maryann's out of the stack and brought it to the teacher's lounge at the lunch break hoping to talk with one of the other teachers she knew owned horses. The other teacher had the same reaction. That essay tugged at her heartstrings too.

"Let me show this to Ginny Hartley, will you?" she asked. "Ginny and her husband own a large ranch in Pinon Hills where I board my horses. She sometimes needs an extra pair of hands. Maybe she'll let Maryann work off some riding lessons in exchange for work around the ranch. This girl needs to become acquainted with a real horse."

The essay and sketch ended up in Ginny's hands that same day. She agreed that the "work for lessons" was a perfect idea. Ginny stopped by Andrews Hardware the next morning and talked with Rose. At first Rose resisted. "I thank you for your offer but we really don't need charity. We are doing just fine."

"No, that's not what I'm offering," Ginny said gently. "It appears you have a horse-crazy daughter and probably can't afford the expense of a horse. What I'm offering is a job for her so she can earn her own lessons. Sometimes, for kids, things like that mean more to them when they earn them themselves."

Rose considered that. "You're right. I think it will mean more to her if she earns it. I agree with you. I'll talk to her tonight when I get home from work. Can I call you later this evening?"

Ginny left her business card with Rose and left the store smiling. If Maryann was as smart as her teachers said she was, she would be a delight to have around the ranch. Ginny could use another pair of hands and she loved teaching youngsters how to ride. Sounded like a win/win to her.

Rose called Ginny later that evening. She told Ginny she was going to have to tie her daughter down to a rock or she would float away on happiness. She was over the moon excited and they would get her to the ranch on Saturday morning. She asked how Maryann should dress and if she should pack her a lunch.

Friday night Maryann had her dream again and she told the Duchess she would see her soon before she woke up. She was dressed and had lunch packed by six in the morning. Rose came to the kitchen for morning coffee and found Maryann almost jumping with excitement to get going. "Hey, you. Slow down and have some breakfast, will you? I promised to have you at the ranch by eight so we have an hour and a half yet before we leave." Maryann finally settled down long enough to eat a bowl of cold cereal, a piece of fruit and drink a tall glass of milk. She was in the car waiting for Rose by 7:30 a.m.

Ginny met them at the gate. She told Rose to pick Maryann up at three that afternoon. "We're usually done with most of the chores by noon and Maryann will have her first horseback lesson after that."

Ginny took her down to the ranch after putting her lunch sack in the refrigerator. She talked with her the whole time telling her what to expect and what was expected from her. When they walked into the first horse stall to check the water level and cleanliness, Maryann stopped and asked, "Can I touch him?"

"Can you touch who?" Ginny asked.

"This horse," Maryann almost whispered. "And can I smell him?"

"Go ahead. This is my gelding Bobbie. He'd be delighted to have you touch him."

Maryann reached out the stroked his neck, bringing her hand back like she was shocked. "It feels so nice! He's so soft. Are they all like that?" She was serious. She reached out and stroked his neck again.

"Yes, this is what a real horse feels like, unless they are dirty," Ginny chuckled. "Haven't you ever petted a horse before?"

"No, this is the first time for real," Maryann said with reverence. "Can I smell him?"

"Of course you can," Ginny grinned. "You'll get used to the smell of horses soon enough."

Maryann pressed her nose to Bobbie's neck and breathed deeply. "Oh, Mrs. Hartley, do they all smell so wonderful?" she asked, pressing her nose in for another smell.

"Well, to start with my name is Ginny. I'm also known as Aunt Ginny, your choice. My mother-in-law was Mrs. Hartley. And, yes, they all smell like that unless they are very dirty or sweaty. You'll get used to it."

"Oh, no, I'll never get enough of it," Maryann smiled at her, "Aunt Ginny."

Brody walked up then. "You need some help?" he asked his aunt.

"Yes, I have some book work I need to do in my office. You know Maryann don't you?"

"Yeah, we have one class together. Good to see you Maryann. Heard you are coming in to give us a hand," Brody smiled at her.

Ginny gave Brody instructions about which horses needed grooming, including water buckets and feeders and left the two in the barn. Brody showed Maryann where to find the grooming supplies and showed her how to brush horses down, curry them, and how to check feed and water buckets. The two of them worked side by side the balance of the morning. They chatted about horses, school, teachers they had, and the coming winter. At noon they walked back to the house. Brody left her on the deck while he went to the kitchen for their lunches. Maryann said she wanted to eat outside so she could see the horses.

Brody walked by his aunt's office on his way back from the kitchen. "I think she's going to work out great, Aunt Ginny. She's smart, she's not a silly girl, and she's a hard worker. We're going to have lunch on the deck then she's all yours for a lesson."

After lunch, Ginny spent the next two and a half hours with Maryann, going over tack, grooming, picking out the horse's feet and lounging him before she mounted. Maryann already knew what each piece of tack was called and how it was used; she'd just never used it before. Ginny demonstrated mounting then walking, trotting and cantering Bobbie in the arena. She helped Maryann mount up and told her where to keep her feet and legs, arms, hands and shoulders, where her chin should be and how she should sit in the saddle. She told her one time and it became set in cement for Maryann. Maryann walked Bobbie for a few laps, then cued him to trot. She sat his trot perfectly. She did several laps in both directions before cueing him on to a canter. She looked like she had been riding horses since she could walk. She was completely comfortable in the saddle even though this was her first time in one. Ginny was dumbstruck. She had a real, live phenomenon in front of her. Ginny's wheels began to spin. What this girl could accomplish was unlimited. Give her a horse and she would ride the hair right off of it. That was an old expression her daddy used when he watched an accomplished rider. Her daddy would have been as excited about Maryann as she was now.

At the end of the day, when Rose came to get her, Maryann was tired. But it was a good tired, the kind you get when you finish a job well. Some of her craving for horses was satisfied a tiny bit. She knew there was more to come and she couldn't wait to get back to it. Rose and Ginny set up a schedule for Maryann that wouldn't impact her ability to get her homework done and still gave her time to ride. Aunt Adele or Uncle Roy could drop her off after school and Rose would pick her up on her way home from work. Maryann had the best night's sleep ever and she spent time with the Duchess in the moonlight again.

CHAPTER FOUR

Maryann quickly fell into a routine. She carried work clothes and an after school snack in her backpack and left a pair of work shoes in a plastic bag in the car. She ran from her last class of the day to meet Uncle Roy or Aunt Adele and could hardly wait to get to the ranch to start working. She especially loved grooming horses. She curried and brushed and picked hooves. She checked water buckets, dumped and cleaned messy ones, refilled them and rehung them where needed. She checked feeders for cleanliness. Ginny showed her how to saddle-soap tack so she stripped down bridles, cleaned them thoroughly, reassembled them and rehung them in the tack room. She polished saddles until they gleamed. She was thorough, organized and happy. Brody worked with her when he wasn't helping Uncle Mike on the other side of the ranch. Ginny couldn't believe how nice her tack room looked in just one month. The floor was always swept and clean, tack organized, brushes and combs cleaned and put away.

Every Wednesday and Saturday Maryann had a riding lesson on Bobbie. For Ginny, it was not so much a lesson as it was just to remind her of what she already knew. Within the first month Maryann and Bobbie were a competitive team. They were as good as any of the other girls Ginny taught, some of whom had been coming to the ranch for lessons for several years.

Bobbie hadn't shown for years. Ginny used him as her lesson horse for new riders because he was so calm and well trained. He also had a knack for knowing when a new rider was losing their balance. He would stop and give them time to adjust before proceeding. After watching Bobbie and Maryann for a month, Ginny thought it was time to get them in the show ring together. She decided to change up the format of the Wednesday lesson to give her students some different things to think about besides correct leads and posting on the right diagonal.

Ginny gathered her five students together in the barn and told them what she had in mind. Rather than individual lessons, they would have a group lesson to practice show ring skills. "I'd like you to gather at the in-gate as a group and then one at a time enter the arena like you're going before a judge. Come in brilliant, at a perfect hunter trot and smile like you are having the time of your life. This is your only chance to make a good first impression on the judge. I will stand in the middle of the arena and observe you like a judge will. I will call for change of direction and change of gaits. We're getting you ready for an accredited All Arabian show in a month. Let's pretend we're doing it today."

Maryann, Susie, Heidi, Melissa and Kathy finished getting their horses ready to ride, then mounted and rode to the arena gate. Brody opened it for them and they filed in, one by one, at their best hunter trot. Ginny corrected mistakes as they occurred, suggested ways to remain in the open, not bunched in a group, change gait and change direction. At the end of the "class" Ginny had them line up down the center

27

of the arena and wait quietly for the judge's decisions like they would in a show class. She talked to each girl, giving her suggestions for making her performance better. She was pleased with all five of them.

"That's it for today, ladies. Great class, all of you. You can go take care of your horses now." Ginny announced.

The girls filed out of the arena and went back to the barn to untack their horses. The clique ignored Maryann completely. They whispered among themselves in the barn aisle but Maryann overheard some of the conversation. "She's not showing. She doesn't even have show- clothes to wear." "SHE doesn't have a horse either." "What's she doing here anyway?" "Yeah. Her MOMMY can't afford to send her to a show. Why is Ginny wasting her time on HER?"

Maryann took care of Bobbie, curried and brushed him down, picked his feet and walked him back to his stall. She hugged him and thanked him for a good ride and gave him pieces of apple she'd brought with her as a treat for him. Her face burned with embarrassment from the comments she'd overheard. Tears welled in her eyes. She spoke to no one. When she cleaned and returned Ginny's tack to the tack room, she walked out of the barn to begin her chores.

Brody caught up with her a few minutes later and noticed right off that she wasn't her usual cheerful self. "Hey, what's up with you today?" he asked.

Maryann turned her head and quickly wiped a tear from her eye before speaking. "It's … it's nothing, really," she answered and continued scrubbing the water bucket in her hands.

Brody walked up to her and took the bucket. "This is not like you. Really! Tell me what's wrong," he asked quietly.

Maryann reluctantly told Brody what she'd overheard in the barn. She begged him not to say anything about it. Brody leaned back against the pipe rail in the stall and looked at her. "Are you kidding me? Did you see yourself out there? I did! You were the best rider in that arena and you're riding Aunt Ginny's 22-year-old gelding making them look like a bunch of rank amateurs. I don't care how much money their parents have. They shouldn't be talking about you or anyone else like that. Those girls need a lesson, but it's not a riding lesson."

Maryann thanked Brody for his concern and took the bucket back to finish scrubbing. "Just don't make a big deal out of it, will ya? That would only make things worse." She continued with her chores and didn't say another word about it.

Brody, on the other hand, was incensed about the way the other girls talked about Maryann. Who did they think they were anyway? Over dinner that night he told Ginny all about his conversation with Maryann that day. Ginny's jaw clenched when Brody repeated some of the comments Maryann overhead in the barn. "Well, I wasn't expecting that. I WILL, however, take care of it and it won't happen again or they will need to find another trainer. I won't stand for bullying on this ranch."

The next day all four of the girls came over to ride, Ginny called them together in the barn. "I heard what you girls said about Maryann after our last lesson. Let me tell you a few things. Maryann has been riding for one month, not two years, not two and a half years, not three years or more like you girls. She outrode every one of you! She didn't use the wrong diagonal twice like you did Melissa. Heidi, she didn't take six strides to change from trot to canter like you did, and you did that three times. She didn't stop her horse for the halt like a reining horse sliding the way you did every time, Susie. Kathy, she didn't deliberately cut you off the way you did her. She managed her horse with dignity and class. You should all be ashamed of yourselves! This is supposed to be fun. It's not fun if you attack each other. There will be no further bullying on my ranch or the bully will have to go somewhere else. Is that clear to all of you?"

All four girls were studying the toes of their riding boots when Ginny finished. Each of them was embarrassed and ashamed. Heidi was the first to speak up. "Ginny, I'm so sorry. It won't happen again." The other three joined in apologizing.

"Well, I'm happy to put that behind us," Ginny said and smiled at the group. "Now, I have something to ask of you. You girls are right about a few things. Maryann's mother can't afford new clothes for her to show in so I'm looking for some you don't use or have outgrown so we can help outfit her for the show next month. Are you willing to help?"

All of them had clothes they didn't use, had outgrown, or spares they were willing to loan. In five minutes, Maryann had a complete outfit pledged. Ginny was so pleased. She asked them to keep this to themselves until she had a chance to talk to Maryann and her mother. She wanted it to be a surprise. All the girls agreed. They couldn't wait to get on with their lesson and requested they use the same format as last time. They needed practice riding with each other to get ready for the big show and they wanted Maryann in the arena with them.

CHAPTER FIVE

One week after Sara Evans left the Pinon Hills cabin in a panic, a 16-year-old dirt-bike rider came to the top of the rise looking down at the cabin and saw something out of the ordinary. He saw Reilly Stone's body lying where it fell, head down and feet up on the steps. The smell reached all the way to where he stopped his bike.

He pulled out his cell phone and dialed "911." When the dispatcher came on the line, he described the scene in front of him and gave her his location, including the GPS coordinates off his phone. He promised the dispatcher he would stay right where he was and would flag down the patrol car when it got close to him. And he promised not to go closer or touch anything. That was easy, his stomach was queasy from the smell at this distance, two hundred feet away. He hoped the breeze would change direction before the Deputies got there.

A single Deputy Sheriff arrived shortly and took the witness statement from the kid and let him go on about his business. He drove his patrol car to the cabin and looked at the bloated corpse, noted the impossible angle of his head from his neck and surmised the man had accidently fallen down the steps. He called it in to his Watch Commander. There was no need for paramedics. The Watch Commander sent several people to the scene to collect any evidence, including Detective Sam Brown who was the Lead on the case. Sam looked over the scene when he got there and noticed the broken whiskey bottles, beer cans and trash around the cabin. He also looked through the still open front door and saw the same inside. There wasn't much speculation in this case. It was pretty obvious to everyone the man drank himself into a stupor and fell off the porch backwards, breaking his neck in the process. This was an accidental death. The Sheriff's photographer took photos of the body where and when found, a few photos outside of the cabin and one or two just inside the door before putting his camera away. Sam Brown called the Coroner to pick up the body and waited until his people arrived with the Coroner's van.

Sam found the wallet in Reilly Stone's rear pocket and took it for evidence. He gave the name on the driver's license to the coroner's people. The driver's license photo was a close enough match to the body no one felt they needed further identification. As soon as the body was loaded in the coroner's van, Sam Brown wiped the eucalyptus salve from his nose with a tissue. That was the only thing he found that helped keep the smell of death from making him sick. Sam wrote pertinent information in a new case file, closed the front door of the cabin and taped it with crime scene tape. As far as he was concerned, that closed this case. He drove back to the office to look up next of kin so he could do the notification. That was almost the worst part of his job. He hated being the bearer of bad news, especially to the loved ones.

From the time Sara Evans got back home from the cabin in Pinon Hills, she was a nervous wreck. She went inside her home and checked the locks on every door and window. Then she checked them all again and did it multiple times each day. All the blinds and draperies were drawn so no one could see in the house. She was in constant fear that Reilly Stone would show up at her door. Even the phone ringing made her jump. She took a hot shower when she got home that night, but was afraid to get in the shower again in case Reilly did show up. She kept the lights off in the front of the house so people wouldn't realize there was someone home.

Sara had a nasty bruise on her left cheekbone from the slap Reilly gave her. In a couple of days, it turned her eye black and blue as well. She put ice packs on the bruise for several days to reduce the swelling. She also had large bruises on her neck from where Reilly tried to strangle her. Her right knee was bruised and scraped where she tried to knee him with it. She was one big mess and couldn't stop crying. She didn't sleep well. She wasn't hungry. She wandered the big old house in the dark, unable to sit still for any length of time. She wore a high turtleneck sweater to cover the bruises on her neck and long pants to cover the bruises on her knee. She kept a pair of dark glasses with her just in case.

When the knock did finally come on her door a little over a week later, she almost jumped out of her skin. She peeked out through the living room draperies and saw a San Bernardino County Sheriff's car in her driveway. Her heart almost stopped. She made her way to the door on shaky legs and peeked through the peephole to find two men standing at her door. One was in uniform and the other in a plain dark blue suit. Her mind whirled. If she didn't answer maybe they'd just go away, but would that look suspicious? She hadn't done anything wrong! Her hand reached toward the doorknob several times and she pulled it back, afraid. Afraid of what? She finally opened the door. Her voice cracking, she asked "What can I do for you?"

"We are looking for Anne Stone. Is she at home?" Sam Brown asked.

"I'm sorry, no she's not. She passed away two and a half months ago," Sara answered.

"Are you a relative?" Sam inquired.

"Yes, I'm Anne's niece. Why were you looking for her?"

"We're looking for relatives of Reilly Stone. Are you related to him?" Sam asked her.

"He would be my uncle by marriage, I guess," Sara told him. "Reilly had no other relatives that I know of."

"In that case, may we come in for a minute? We have some news for you," Sam explained.

Sara opened the front door and the two men filed in. She showed them to the living room and switched on one of the side lamps. That only slightly brightened the dark room.

Once the three were all in the living room, Sam suggested, "Please take a seat. We have some bad news for you. May we sit down?"

Sara nodded and sat in her favorite comfy chair while the officer and the detective sat on the couch.

"Ma'am, we're here to tell you Reilly Stone was in an accident. It was fatal. It appears that he's been dead for about a week. It looks like he fell down the steps at his cabin and broke his neck. We're sorry to have to bring you such bad news," Sam began. He watched Sara closely for her reaction. As an officer, reactions to this kind of news were unpredictable. She looked more relieved than anything. That surprised him and put up a flicker of a red flag in his mind.

"Oh, so he finally did it? He's been a notorious heavy drinker for some time. I often wondered how long it would take him to kill himself with that stuff. I just hoped he wouldn't be driving and take some poor innocent person with him," Sara finally said out loud. She felt like a heavy burden had just been lifted off her shoulders. She took a deep breath, the first one she had taken in over a week.

"Yes, ma'am. His blood alcohol was very high. It does appear alcohol contributed to his accident. His body is at the coroner's office now awaiting autopsy, but our preliminary findings are that his death was accidental. Is there anyone else we should notify?" Sam asked her.

"In all the years my aunt was married to him, she never met a relative of his, only his drinking buddies or his golfing buddies, and not many of them. They lived separate lives for a long, long time. I never understood why Aunt Annie didn't divorce him. He disappeared for months and sometimes years at a time and never communicated with her. He showed up on occasion, sometimes for just a night and sometimes for a few days or weeks then disappeared again. He never told her where he was or where he went. It was the strangest marriage I ever saw."

"I know this has to be a bad time for you. Here's my business card. If you have any questions, you can reach me on my direct number there," Sam said, standing and holding out his business card to her.

"Well, there is one thing," Sara said. "My aunt made me the sole heir in her will, this house for example. She also left me that horse," she pointed at the photograph of La Duquesa over the fireplace. "She left me a small cabin in Pinon Hills too. Aunt Annie died of cancer. I was her only living relative, besides Uncle Reilly, and we've been very close since my parents died right after I finished high school. I quit my job to care for her. We lived at the cabin because she could bring her horse there and see her every day. When Aunt Annie died I called Tania, her horse trainer, to pick the horse up and get her safely back into Tania's training barn while I sorted things out here. I didn't find out until about a week ago that Tania showed up to get the horse and Uncle Reilly chased her off. He must have gotten to the cabin sometime after I left that day. I asked him what he did with the horse, because Aunt Annie left her to me in her will. All he would tell me is that he sold her. That horse was Aunt Annie's prized possession. I'm worried about her. I have no idea how to find her. Would you happen to know a private investigator I could hire to do that?"

"As a matter of fact one of my best friends left the department and went out on his own doing private investigations. He's the one I would want on my case. His name is Charles Spade. I'll jot his number down on the back of my business card," Sam told her as he took the card back from Sara and jotted a phone number and name on the back of it. "Give Charlie a call and tell him Sam sent you. He'll do a good job for you."

Sara escorted the two to the front door and thanked them again for their kindness. When she shut the door, she leaned her back against it and cried again. This time she was crying from sheer relief.

CHAPTER SIX

Maryann and Brody became good friends. Maryann worked at the ranch after school and on Saturdays. They were only a year apart in age and they found they had many things in common. When Brody wasn't working with Uncle Mike, he was helping Maryann with her chores. They laughed, splashed each other from water buckets, and sat in the barn aisle talking about horses while they cleaned tack. Clyde, being a Labrador retriever, was always in on the splashing parts. He loved the water. Occasionally Ginny let them ride together on short trail rides with Clyde along. Brody always watched Maryann's lessons if he wasn't busy. She was such a talented rider, he enjoyed the show.

Brody was almost as excited as Maryann was when Ginny told her she would be competing in the next All Arabian Show. Maryann couldn't believe her ears when Ginny told her all the show clothes she needed were donated or loaned by the other girls and they asked for her to ride with them during their group lessons. She made a point of thanking each of them and assured them any of the loans would be returned after the show, cleaned and ready to use again.

Rose agreed to it after Ginny explained that Maryann was going to ride her horse Bobbie so Ginny would be paying all the show fees. Roy and Adele chipped in for Maryann's food at the show grounds so there wasn't anything left for Rose to pay for.

Brody was the second one in the family to discover Maryann's artistic talents. She showed him some of her work in art class. He was amazed at how lifelike her drawings and paintings of the horses were. He loved her painting of Bobbie which Maryann planned to give Ginny as a thank you after the show.

The day of the show, all five girls drove to the show grounds with parents or Ginny in packed SUVs and trucks pulling two trailers for the five horses. They took all the tack, gear, and feed for the horses they needed for four days. The girls planned to sleep in the tack room at the show so they could be close to their horses. They brought cots, blankets, sleeping bags, coolers and overnight bags for their shower gear. They'd shower at the show grounds before and after each day's classes. All their show clothes were cleaned, pressed and ready.

The show was a whirlwind of excitement for Maryann. There were so many beautiful horses to see and watch perform in every discipline. She rode Bobbie to warm him up before her classes and rode him perfectly in each class. She stood on the rail when the other girls were in their classes watching and cheering them on. The girls all helped each other get into show clothes, get their horses ready and get to the arena in time. The team worked like a well-oiled machine. There was just so much to see and do! At the end of the show Maryann brought home blue ribbons for each of her classes. There were a large number of firsts, seconds and thirds among all the girls. Ginny was pleased with the performance of her team. Maryann was completely hooked.

Rose, Aunt Adele and Uncle Roy searched for used tack sales and bought items for Maryann so she could have her own things. They also purchased used show clothes. Christmas that year was all about the horse. All of Maryann's Christmas gifts had something to do with horses. She got her own tack box filled with her own brushes, curry, sweat scraper, mane and tail combs and a really cute hook pick made from an old horse shoe by an enterprising farrier. Rose saved up and bought her a new pair of paddock boots to wear at the barn because her old tennis shoes were wearing out. They doubled as her riding boots.

Horse shows continued after the first of the year about a month apart. Ginny spent time with Maryann teaching her a new discipline on Bobbie. He was as good a Western horse as he was a Hunter. It didn't take her long to excel as a Western rider. Brody brought out some of the obstacles used in Trail classes. She practiced with Bobby going over the wooden bridge, going through a free standing gate, and walking in patterns over poles.

The work continued through the winter even though the weather was cold and water often froze in water buckets. Horse bathing was done inside the barn with warm water and the horses were dried in their stalls in coolers instead of using the hot walker in the sunshine. Snow came and went but there was usually enough sunshine during the shorter afternoons to get some riding in before dusk. The only thing Maryann wished for was a horse of her own. She never told anyone about that because she knew her mother could never afford the expense. She was happy Ginny let her use Bobbie.

One Saturday in late March, she came to the ranch and Brody met her at the gate excited about a horse that walked onto the ranch late in the afternoon the day before. He took her to the barn and showed him to her. The poor horse looked plenty worse for wear. He was terribly thin and had wounds all over his back, hips and sides. Brody told her Uncle Mike thought the horse might have been attacked by a mountain lion. Aunt Ginny had been gone for a couple of weeks. She and a friend of hers were staying in San Juan Capistrano taking care of Arabian horses for friends of theirs. It was sad. The couple's daughter was in a coma in a hospital and her parents wanted to stay with her. Becky Howard was the same age as Maryann, so she could relate to that. She'd want her mother with her if she was in the hospital too.

Uncle Mike and Brody were running the ranch without Aunt Ginny's help. With all the extra work, Uncle Mike asked Brody to take care of the stray horse. Maryann offered to help Brody with that. She helped him clean the stallion's stall, helped clean his wounds and put salve in the open sores. She helped him prepare small buckets of soaked feed to get his metabolism working again and gain some weight. She helped Brody brush him down and keep him clean.

When Uncle Mike asked Brody to put flyers together about the horse so they could put them in local feed stores to try and find his owner, Brody asked Maryann for help. She was much more artistic than he was. The two managed to get a couple of photos for the flyer. She designed it to attract attention so more people would look at it. While working with the horse, Brody and Maryann came to know just what a nice horse he was even if he was a stallion. He was sweet, kind and gentle. He "talked" to them every time they came into the barn. He also seemed to like Clyde for some reason, always nickering to him when Clyde followed them into the barn. Several times they caught Clyde whining at the horse and the horse nickering back at Clyde like they were in a conversation. As Brody and Maryann worked with the horse, his appearance improved. Maryann thought he was a really beautiful Arabian horse.

Five days after the stray horse appeared at the ranch, Maryann ran into a flurry of news people and TV crews at the gate when Uncle Roy dropped her off. She couldn't imagine what that was all about until Brody pulled her aside. "You'll never guess who the stray horse really is," he said. "That horse is Prince Ali, the million dollar stallion!"

"No! Not the horse who's been all over TV and in the papers?" she exclaimed.

"Yup, that's him. I answered the phone last night when Aunt Ginny called and told her about our stray horse. Aunt Ginny came home with her friend Sharon and identified him. Do you believe it?"

"Wow! Well, we knew he was special. I just didn't expect that. Any idea how he got here?" she asked.

"Today has been crazy!" Brody told her. "I didn't go to school at all. Reporters started showing up here right after breakfast. You know Uncle Mike. He doesn't say much. He was overwhelmed with people asking questions so I volunteered to stay home and give him a hand. We've had the Sheriffs up here, TV crews and newspaper people all day. There was an old guy who bought him for a few hundred bucks that showed up with a Deputy. The guy lives way up in the Angeles National Forest. Uncle Mike says it is at least 70 miles as the crow flies from here. That's way up there," Brody pointed toward the South West along the mountain chain.

"How in the heck did he get all the way here?" Maryann puzzled.

"Aunt Ginny also told me that Becky is waking up," Brody told her. "That's why Aunt Ginny's been gone. Becky's parents have been staying with her at the hospital since it all happened taking care of their horses. Maybe she'll be home soon."

"Is that Becky Howard?" Maryann asked.

"Yeah, Aunt Ginny was coaching her and Prince Ali. Becky wants to ride him at Youth Nationals this July. Don't know what's going to happen with that, though. You'll probably get to meet Becky soon. When she gets well enough, she's going to want to see Ali. They've been best friends forever. You'll like her. She's a neat girl, not stuck up or anything. You'd never know her parents are rich."

Brody caught a signal from Uncle Mike. It looked like a couple of reporters were trying to sneak down to the barn again. "Come on, let's get to the barn. We're trying to keep the reporters from blinding Ali with the flash on their cameras. He's been photographed all day. We may have to take him out of his stall," Brody explained as he and Maryann hurried to the main barn.

Brody and Maryann spent the balance of the afternoon entertaining reporters. When Rose came to pick Maryann up, she had to wait until they finished up with water buckets and gave Prince Ali his evening bucket of soaked feed. On their way home, Maryann told her all about her afternoon with the million dollar stallion.

The whole next week was taken up by "lookie-loos" who stopped by the ranch for a peek at Prince Ali. Brody and Maryann spent time grooming him and cleaning his stall while talking with strangers about him. Prince Ali, on his part, was gracious with people and all the attention that focused on him. He made steady progress healing and gaining weight. Finally Uncle Mike told them he could be turned out for an hour to stretch his legs. He put on quite a show with roll-backs at the arena rail, flying lead changes, and that wonderful high floating trot of his. Ali had a "joie de vivre" that was as contagious as the common cold. No one watching him could help but smile.

Maryann was sad the day Prince Ali left to go back home with Becky and her parents. She was going to miss him terribly. Becky couldn't have been nicer. She was truly thankful for the work Brody and Maryann did with Prince Ali while he was in their care. They all swapped cell phone numbers and promised to keep up to date on him. Becky told them she still hoped to compete with Ali at the Youth Nationals in July but was restricted from riding for the next month. She was worried about getting Ali back in shape to compete and didn't know if there was enough time to get herself and her horse ready. Maryann volunteered to do whatever she could to help. That became the beginning of a lasting friendship between Becky and Maryann.

La Duquesa arrived at Hartley Ranch the Sunday following Prince Ali's departure. Aunt Ginny put her in Ali's empty stall in the main barn. Brody volunteered to work with her the same way he worked with Prince Ali. But the two horses came from very different situations. Ali had not been beaten and starved for months.

Ginny fed the mare breakfast Monday morning, petted and talked to her before leaving for other chores. The man who normally cleaned the barn stalls every morning opened Quesa's stall and walked in with his muck rake in his hand. La Duquesa went wild. She tried to go over the stall wall to get away and did her best to go through it when that didn't work. It startled the man and he backed quickly out of the stall, closing and locking it before charging off to find Ginny.

Ginny rushed back to the barn with the man and saw La Duquesa standing in the corner of the stall shaking. "Put a red rope around the stall handle here," she told him as she slowly slid the door open and stepped inside the stall. The mare flinched a little and then stood shaking. When the man was out of her sight, Ginny began talking to the mare in low soothing tones until she calmed down. Quesa finally walked over to Ginny and rested her head on Ginny's shoulder. "No

43

one is going to harm you here," Ginny assured her while stroking her neck. Ginny thought about what happened. When horses are frightened, their "fight or flight" instinct takes over. Those that "fight" are the hardest to deal with. Ginny knew the "flight" could be handled with time and patience. Ginny cleaned her stall that morning.

Brody called Maryann Sunday night and told her about the new horse that arrived that day. He told her about what a mess she was and how skinny she was. She was worse than Prince Ali when he arrived and she was covered in welts from a beating. It broke Maryann's heart to hear about any horse being abused like that. She met Brody at the gate Monday after school and they walked to the barn together with Clyde.

The horse picked up her head when she heard the three of them walk into the barn. She looked directly at Maryann when they came into her view. Maryann stood looking directly into her eyes. Her heart stopped in her chest and she couldn't breathe.

It was HER! How could this be? She stood staring at the Duchess! She was not the beautiful silver white horse in her dreams, she was a mess. But Maryann knew instantly she was looking at the Duchess she'd ridden in the moonlight so many, many times. How could anyone do this to HER? When her heart began beating again, it felt like it was broken. Tears slipped unconsciously down her cheeks. She couldn't tear her eyes away.

"Hey, I was talking to you," Brody said, looking at her curiously.

Maryann turned her head and wiped the tears away with the back of her hand. "I'm sorry. I, uh, I was just shocked looking at her. How could anyone do that to her? I don't understand. She's a beautiful soul and she didn't deserve this."

"I don't know how you can see a beautiful soul in there. She's awful looking right now," Brody answered.

"Look into her eyes," Maryann told him "that's where the beauty is."

CHAPTER SEVEN

Maryann spotted the short section of red rope tied to the stall door handle on La Duquesa's stall. "What is that all about?" she asked Brody.

"Oh, that's just a signal we use around the ranch. If there's a horse Aunt Ginny or Uncle Mike don't want anyone else in the stall with, they tie a red rope around the door handle. They're pretty serious about that too. I've seen it a few times on some of Uncle Mike's stallions in training. If the horse is unpredictable or pushy, they tie a red rope there. Nobody else is to go in that stall without Uncle Mike or Aunt Ginny."

"Why would they tie one on this mare's stall?" Maryann asked.

"I don't have any idea. Guess we'll have to ask Aunt Ginny," Brody told her.

Aunt Ginny walked in the barn just then. Brody asked her about the red rope. She explained what happened that morning when the grounds-man tried to clean the stall. "I was afraid the mare would hurt herself or anyone else who happened to walk in that stall," she explained. "She's been a victim of abuse. Horses like that can be unpredictable so I

don't like to take chances. I'll be cleaning her stall myself.
You kids can give her the soaked feed, but I don't want either
of you to go in there unless I'm with you until we get to know
her better. I can't take a chance she could hurt herself or
accidently hurt you."

Maryann was sad. There was nothing she wanted more
than to get close to the real live Duchess. She didn't say
anything about it to anyone. She never defied authority in
her life. If her mother said "no", it was "no." If her teacher
asked her for something, she did her best to give it to her.
She never bucked Aunt Adele or Uncle Roy. But she had to
find a way to spend private time with her Duchess. Late that
night, she came up with an idea. She tucked a well-worn
copy of Black Beauty in her school backpack and crawled
into bed. She dreamed she rode the silver white mare across
a grassy meadow in the light of the moon.

The next afternoon, Maryann looked for an opportunity.
Uncle Mike called Brody to the other side of the ranch and
Aunt Ginny was in her office doing paperwork. Maryann slid
the book out of her backpack and slipped into La Duquesa's
stall, keeping her back against the wall until she came to
the corner. She slid down underneath the corner feeder
and opened the book on her knees. She began to read out
loud. La Duquesa stood in the opposite corner of the stall,
shaking at first. In a few minutes, she seemed to realize the
little person in her stall presented no threat to her and began
to relax. The sound of Maryann's voice was soothing and
melodic. La Duquesa became curious about her, as if she
knew her from somewhere but couldn't remember where.

Maryann didn't want to risk being caught past the red
rope so she stayed only a few minutes in the stall. She slipped
out the same way she slipped in. She bookmarked her place
in Black Beauty and tucked it back in her backpack and

resumed her chores, stopping by to look in on La Duquesa as often as she could.

The second day Maryann slipped into La Duquesa's stall with her book, the mare took a step and a half in her direction before Maryann slipped out and went on with her chores. The third time, the mare came even closer. Less than a week later the mare began nudging the book in Maryann's hands as she read. Maryann took one hand off the book and touched La Duquesa on the nose and cheek. The mare didn't pull away. Maryann was thrilled to be able to touch her at last. She looked at her watch and realized she spent twenty minutes in the stall. She slipped out as quietly as she could, watching the mare as she went. She walked straight into Ginny.

"Well, well, what do we have here?" Ginny asked frowning. "I thought you knew what that red rope was all about, didn't you?"

Maryann stood staring at her boots. "I just wanted to get to know her," Maryann sputtered with tears streaming down her cheeks.

"I put that red rope up to protect that horse AND you, you know," Ginny replied. "She's been hurt enough and I can't take chances with your life either. How would I explain that to your mother if she'd spun around in fear and knocked you down? Really, now how do you think I would feel if you got hurt in there?"

"I'm so sorry, Aunt Ginny. Really. I thought I was helping her," Maryann cried softly.

La Duquesa stuck her head out the feeder door and nickered. Ginny walked over to her and tried to stroke her neck. The mare stared at Maryann and ignored Ginny, pulling away from her.

"Maryann, she seems to be asking for you. Come over here and stroke her neck," Ginny said, watching carefully as

Maryann did what she asked. La Duquesa stood quietly as Maryann stroked her neck and cheek. She closed her eyes obviously enjoying the contact.

"Well, I'll be darned," Ginny said. "I had no idea you were a 'horse whisperer!' If that doesn't beat all!" she smiled at Maryann. "I think you've found a way to open her heart again. I'm going to leave the red rope up for a while and I'd prefer to be here when you go in her stall, but it looks like she's found a friend in you."

"Do you mean it, Aunt Ginny" Maryann perked up. "I'd love to curry her and brush some of that yuck off her. She'll feel so much better. Then maybe we can give her a bath. She needs it more than any horse on this ranch."

Ginny laughed. "Yes I mean it. Let's give it a try, shall we?"

Maryann hurried to the tack room and pulled out her grooming kit. She returned to La Duquesa's stall and brought the kit inside with her. Ginny watched from outside the stall as Maryann began currying the mare from ears to tail. She brushed off the loosened hair and muck as she went along. La Duquesa stood quietly as she worked, flinching occasionally when Maryann hit a sore spot where a bad whip welt had been. Once she finished brushing her, she picked up her combs and began working on the tangle of mane and tail, working from the forelock back. La Duquesa still needed a bath but she looked so much better after the brushing. She nuzzled Maryann as though she were asking her to brush more.

"What do you think, Aunt Ginny?"

"I think you have yourself a new job is what I think. She needs to gain weight but she does look happier that she did before you brushed her down. Maybe we can bath her tomorrow when you get here."

Maryann hugged Ginny when she came out of the stall. "Thank you so much. You have no idea how happy you made me." She hurried to put her grooming kit away and get her other chores done.

The barn was empty when Clyde wandered in. He saw La Duquesa following Maryann with her eyes. *"Hey there, Good Looking!"* Clyde said to get her attention.

"Oh, hello there. How are you getting around these days?" she asked him.

"I'm just an old dog. I get achy hips and knees like any other old thing but life is pretty good here, like I told you when you arrived," the dog answered. He sat and scratched an itchy place behind his ear then asked, *"You never did finish your story. How did you end up in the fix you were in when I found you?"*

"Going back to what I originally told you, I was only two and a half months old when I was taken from my mother. The couple who moved me had no interest in me. I was left alone most of the time but became friends with their old golden retriever and a pair of goats. When I was almost three, Tania came to see me and she took me to her training barn to learn things."

"That's a long time to be ignored," Clyde said. *"Didn't they pay any attention to you?"*

"I got fed twice a day, saw the farrier every two months and the vet came to check me once a year and poke me with something that hurt. Other than that, no. But things were different at Tania's. It was nice. She was nice. She taught me lots of things and we began riding together. It was fun. Then she took me to a horse show. I got a blue ribbon. The couple that owned me got very excited over a silly piece of ribbon. They had Tania show me again at a bigger show and I won a bigger blue ribbon. A really nice lady saw me at that show. I don't know how it happened but she suddenly became my owner. She spent lots of time with me and really loved me. I thought I had found my one-and-only human at last. But she died. That horrible man showed up at the place where I was staying. When he drank too much, he got mean. He used to come to my corral and turn the hose on me.

It was cold outside and I thought I would freeze to death. My corral was always full of mud from him spraying me with water. When he wasn't spraying me he was hitting me with his whip. I couldn't get away from him. He didn't feed me much and he hardly ever filled up my water trough. I had to drink that stinky stuff all the way to the bottom. If you hadn't come along, I'd probably not be here now. You and the nice people you brought with you saved my life so I owe you. Thank you, dear Clyde. You will be my friend for life."

"Oh, Pretty Lady, it was nothing. I could get away from him. Good thing for him I didn't have a chance to take a bite out of him that day!" Clyde said thoughtfully. "I can't image how people could treat a horse the way you were treated. But you don't have to worry any more. These people are really good to their horses. Ginny, the woman, really loves them and I'm sure she will love you dearly when she gets to know you better."

"Can I ask you a question?" La Duquesa asked Clyde.

"Sure, anything."

"Who is that little person who shows up most days here? She's the one who brushed me down. It felt wonderful. I feel as though I know her, but can't remember."

"You must mean Maryann. She comes here after school to help Ginny in exchange for riding lessons. I don't think her mom can afford to pay and I've never heard her mention a dad, so maybe she doesn't have one. She's nice. I like her a lot." Clyde told her.

Clyde spied a squirrel creeping toward the hay shed and took off barking like a banshee. It was, after all, his job to keep the rodent population at bay, or at least off the property.

About a month into her rehabilitation, La Duquesa had gained weight and her silver white coat shined from Maryann's constant grooming. She felt better than she had for months. She'd been turned out a few times to stretch her legs. Her elegant dancing trot across the arena turned heads on the ranch. She was looking beautiful, although still a little thin from her ordeal.

Ginny told Maryann it was time to find out what she knew and what training she'd had. Ginny hauled her saddle to the arena and set it down on the top rail. She put La Duquesa in cross ties in the barn aisle and fitted her with a bridle and walked her to the arena. Ginny free-lounged her both directions for a couple of minutes then saddled her. Maryann hung on the top rail watching with interest. Ginny put her foot in the stirrup and applied a little pressure. La Duquesa stood quietly, not moving a muscle. Ginny went ahead and mounted her and asked her to walk off. La Duquesa set her head in just the right position and walked off perfectly at ease. Ginny walked her several times in both directions and cued her to trot. La Duquesa's trot was like dancing on air, light and floating. Ginny posted easily as they moved one direction, then the other. She cued her to a canter. Ginny felt like she was riding her couch. It was the most comfortable canter she'd ever ridden. She made one pass and asked her to halt. La Duquesa stepped from the canter to a halt in two steps without raising an inch of dust in the arena. Ginny walked her back to the rail where Maryann was watching. "She is wonderful. I can't believe how well trained she is, and she has the best attitude I've ever experienced. She actually likes the work, maybe even loves it."

Maryann's eyes were glued to the horse. She couldn't look away. There was something she desperately wanted to try. "Can I ride her for a minute?" she asked Ginny.

Ginny dismounted and handed the reins to Maryann. "Sure, I know you will love it as much as I did."

Maryann climbed over the rail and pulled the saddle off the horse. "What are you doing?" Ginny asked with concern. She was about to intervene, but something stopped her.

"Please let me try something." Maryann said over her shoulder as she pulled the bridle off the horse as well. She grabbed a small hunk of mane and walked La Duquesa to the rail and positioned her parallel to it. She climbed on the rail and mounted the horse bareback, kicking off her boots. Ginny was about to protest again when Maryann walked off on the mare and settled herself gently on her back. She cued La Duquesa to trot and sat the trot as if she were part of the horse. She guided the mare with her legs and a single hunk of mane in her hand.

Ginny was spellbound. That young girl had only been riding for a few months. Here, nearing sunset, she was riding bareback as though she and the horse were one being. As the last rays of the sun turned the clouds to pink and rose, Maryann asked La Duquesa to canter. Ginny, now in the center of the arena, watched in awe. She saw Maryann throw her arms straight out from her shoulders, turn her hands palm up and tilt her head backward. She closed her eyes and just felt the horse beneath her. The sunset painted the rest of the picture in glowing jewel tones of golds, pinks and purples.

Ginny stared with open mouth. She was stunned. Suddenly she remembered the essay Maryann wrote so many months ago and the picture she'd drawn to go with it. That was what she was seeing in front of her now except it was sunset, not moonlight that lit the scene. Maryann was even wearing the exact same shirt and pants from that picture, right down to the "L" shaped tear on the left knee and the plaid of the shirt. Ginny had no words.

Maryann slowed La Duquesa to a walk and brought her back to the arena rail so she could dismount. She threw the reins around her neck and walked her back to the barn aisle cross ties so she could brush her down before putting her away in her stall. She hugged the mare and thanked her for such a good ride and handed her a few apple pieces she'd brought with her.

It took Ginny a few minutes to carry the saddle back to the barn tack room. She didn't know what to say.

As she passed beside the horse in cross ties, Maryann asked, "Aunt Ginny, what is this mare's registered name? I don't think I've heard you call her anything but "the mare," so I've been calling her Duchess. That's the name of the horse I've ridden in my dreams since I can remember."

Ginny almost dropped the saddle. She turned and looked at Maryann. "Her registered name is La Duquesa. I thought I'd told you that. "La Duquesa" is Spanish for "The Duchess."

That was the moment Ginny absolutely knew Maryann belonged to La Duquesa and La Duquesa belonged to Maryann. They were meant to be together.

CHAPTER EIGHT

S am Brown was puzzled when he got a message from the
Coroner's office about the Reilly Stone case. He'd closed
that case down almost as soon as it landed on his desk. He'd
gone to the scene, looked it over and chalked the death up
to an accident. He'd even told the next-of-kin that weeks
ago. He called the Coroner's office. The secretary told him
the Coroner needed to speak with him. He had finished the
autopsy on Reilly Stone, gotten the toxicology reports back
and needed to see him. Sam made the appointment and told
his boss.

When Sam arrived for his appointment, he was given a
set of booties, gown and gloves to put on. He was escorted
into an exam room lined with tables. Most of the tables
had bodies on them under sheets. He wished he had his
eucalyptus salve the minute he walked in the room. The
Coroner greeted him and asked him to join him at one of
the tables near the middle of the room.

"I'm sorry to do this to you, but we just finished up
the autopsy on Reilly Stone. On my initial exam, I was in
complete agreement with you. It appeared the guy was

drunk as a skunk and fell off the steps and broke his darned neck. The toxicology report does show his blood alcohol level was almost three times the legal limit so he was definitely impaired."

"Okay, so what have you got for me?" Sam asked.

"We found something strange when we got to looking. The man's neck was broken so badly it severed his spinal cord. It was effectively an internal decapitation. But there was no internal bleeding at the sight. With that much bone and muscle damage there should have been some bleeding. So we looked into it a little more and did some additional x-rays."

"What did they show?"

"Let me show you the x-rays we took," as he pulled them from a sleeve and hung them on a light box. "Just here, you can see the actual cause of death. Do you see that depressed skull fracture? It is just over his ear along the left side of his temple. That's what killed him. We've looked at x-rays from several angles and we looked at the injury to his head. We found bone fragments penetrating the brain. He took a hard blow to his left temple with a large flat object of some kind. We just haven't been able to figure out what it was. There's no trace evidence of the weapon in the injury that we can find."

"Did he get that injury from a fall prior to falling down the stairs?" Sam asked.

"No. There was too much force used to give him the injury to his brain. That couldn't have been done in a fall even with a man his size. It wouldn't generate enough force."

"Okay, Doc. What are you telling me here?"

"I'm afraid I'm telling you this was no accident. I believe this is a homicide. Someone used a heavy flat object to bash his skull in before his body fell down the stairs."

"Oh, great! None of us did much at the scene that day since it looked so obvious to us what happened. We didn't collect much evidence or even look for any." Sam told him.

"Oh, one more thing. I found a strange substance on his clothes and in his hair. It was greasy and it took me a while to figure out what it was. I finally gave it my "smell" test. It was bacon grease! I will tell you we found bacon and eggs in his stomach contents if that helps you."

"Oh, wonderful! The guy eats breakfast while he's getting drunk. Sounds perfect!" Sam muttered under his breath. "Thanks, Doc. We'll see where this takes us."

CHAPTER NINE

Rose showed up to take Maryann home soon after she had her first ride on La Duquesa so Ginny didn't have much time to think or to talk with her. "Maybe that's not such a bad thing," Ginny thought. She didn't say much to either Brody or Mike over dinner. She cleaned up the kitchen afterwards and went in to have a long soak in the tub. That's where she did her best thinking.

First, that five-hundred-dollar horse was no five-hundred-dollar horse. Ginny knew that. All you had to do was take one look at her today. She was still a bit thin, but not bad. She needed muscle tone but that came with proper exercise. Other than that, La Duquesa was one gorgeous mare. She had an elegance in her way of moving, even being walked to the arena for turnout. She held her head proudly as any duchess would. She was gentle and kind and did what was asked of her without argument. She was easily the best horse to deal with Ginny had ever encountered. La Duquesa had class!

Then there was the whole Maryann thing. The way Maryann had turned the mare around from being scared to death of everyone to the gentle lady she was today was remarkable. But she also knew Maryann's mother could never afford to keep a horse for her daughter. She remembered Brody telling her a little about Maryann's background. Rose had talked to Maryann a little about her father. He was killed in an auto accident just before Rose found out she was pregnant. They married against his parents' wishes and he was their only child. They were very wealthy and wanted him to marry someone more their status. They disowned Rose the night her husband died. Rose hadn't had contact with them since. Rose gave up her own education and came west. She was taken in by her father's sister and her husband. They survived on Adele and Roy's social security pension and what Rose earned at the local hardware store. There wasn't much wiggle room in their budget and certainly not enough to care for a horse and a horse-show crazy teenager.

Fortunately for Ginny, she could afford the horse. She could also support the expense of showing the horse. She knew the best person in the world to do that was Maryann. She made up her mind that was what she would do.

The next time Maryann came to the ranch Ginny took her aside. "You will have to learn a new discipline now," she told her. "You've done really well with Bobbie in the Hunter Pleasure classes and the Western Pleasure classes. But La Duquesa is not a hunter or western horse. How do you feel about learning how to ride a Country Pleasure horse in the shows?"

Maryann brightened up. "Do you mean it, Aunt Ginny? Really? Can I ride La Duquesa in the shows?"

Ginny smiled, "Yes, absolutely, but you have to use the flat saddle. You can't ride bareback."

They went to the barn and took La Duquesa out of her stall. Ginny showed Maryann how to tack her up for an English class with the flat saddle and double bridle. "There are two bits used. One is a curb bit, that's the straight solid bar here," Ginny explained. "And you use a snaffle bit, the one with the break in the center like you've been using on Bobbie, only it is a little smaller too."

Maryann examined the bridle before Ginny showed her how to put it on. "This is the same setup we use for Prince Ali," she told her. "He is an English Pleasure horse because he lifts his knees higher so his front legs break over level. La Duquesa doesn't reach level with her front legs so she's a Country Pleasure horse."

Maryann soaked up the instruction like a sponge. She closed her eyes and remembered watching Prince Ali in the turnout. In profile, when he lifted his front leg to move forward, his foreleg was parallel with the ground or a little higher than that. With La Duquesa, she didn't lift the foreleg quite as high, but much higher than Bobbie did as a hunter. Her foreleg was not quite parallel to the ground. She understood the difference.

Correctly saddled and bridled, Ginny led La Duquesa to the arena. She mounted her and began showing Maryann where the horse needed to hold her head and neck. She was much more upright than Bobby was at either hunter or western riding. Ginny showed her how to hold both sets of reins in her hands and how to use the snaffle bit to guide the mare. "You only use the curb bit to check your mare and slow her down," she told her. "I know this is confusing, but I'm here to watch and help." She put in a couple of laps, talking to Maryann constantly about what she was doing as she rode.

Maryann mounted, stroked Quesa's neck and asked her to trot. Maryann copied Ginny's posture and how she held her hands. Her legs naturally fell in just the right place for close contact with La Duquesa's sides. Ginny watched them from the center of the arena. They moved together as if they were one. It was beautiful to watch. Maryann self-corrected when needed and continued. Ginny saw blue ribbons all over that ride. She was pleased.

The lesson continued with Ginny standing in the center of the arena watching. There wasn't anything else for her to do. Maryann and La Duquesa had the look of a pair who'd been together for years. Ginny didn't even see Maryann cueing the horse to change direction or change gait. They did serpentines down the length of the arena with Maryann's legs as the only guide for the horse. Maryann had La Duquesa do small circles to the left and to the right. She did figure eights. La Duquesa's flying lead changes were perfect at the center of the pattern.

Ginny called the lesson a little earlier than she would have normally. La Duquesa was out of shape. She needed the work, but in shorter doses as she built back up. Ginny explained that to Maryann. "It wouldn't be a bad idea to take her on short trail rides with Brody too. All show horses need something other than the inside of an arena to look at."

Maryann was bubbling over when Rose picked her up that night. "Oh, mom, you should have been there! La Duquesa is wonderful to ride. I love her!" Rose began to worry. She didn't have the money to support a horse and the expense of horse showing. It was obvious her little girl wanted that with all her heart. What was she going to do? She'd have to think about it.

Maryann called Becky after dinner. They talked regularly since Prince Ali went home. Maryann wanted updates on how he was doing and how Becky was doing after their tragic separation. Becky reported Prince Ali was completely healed and his hair had grown out enough to cover the scars from the mountain lion attack. "When are you going to ride him again?" Maryann asked.

"My doctor just gave me another two weeks off. He said I am healing well but he wants me to wait a little longer. I've never fallen off Ali! I can't stand this. We are getting closer and closer to the Youth Nationals and I can't ride him to get him in shape either. I don't know what we're going to do," Becky told her.

"How about I talk Aunt Ginny into bringing me to your place so I can ride him for you?" Maryann suggested. "I'm riding Country Pleasure now so I'm sure I could ride him. Would that help?"

"You'd do that for me?" Becky asked. "Wow that would be wonderful! At least we could get him in better shape. Maybe you could come here a couple of times a week. That way you can still ride Quesa and get her ready."

"I didn't think about getting Quesa ready for the Youth Nationals," Maryann admitted. That was an out-of-the-blue suggestion to her. "Do you think I could ride at that competition?"

"Why not?" Becky said. "According to what Aunt Ginny told my mom, you are ready for that. You just needed a good horse. And it sounds like you found her. It would be so much fun to go to that show with you!"

"Oh, really? Then maybe we should talk to our moms and Aunt Ginny. Let's cross our fingers and hope this works," Maryann said in surprise.

CHAPTER TEN

G inny wasn't surprised when Maryann approached her about riding Prince Ali for Becky. That was what she'd come to expect from Maryann. She was always willing to help someone else. As long as it was okay with Caroline Howard and Maryann's mother, Rose, it was fine with her.

Ginny picked Maryann up at school and they drove to San Juan Capistrano. Maryann was surprised at Becky's home. She didn't expect that. It was huge, gorgeous, and they even had a housekeeper. Maryann never knew anyone that had a housekeeper. When Aunt Ginny took her to the barn area to meet Becky, she was surprised all over again. The horse area was beautiful. There were grass pastures with horses turned out in them. The barn was stately. Even the stall door handles were solid brass and highly polished. They spied Becky in the breezeway with Prince Ali in cross ties waiting for them. Becky had him almost ready to ride. Becky hugged Aunt Ginny and thanked her for bringing Maryann to ride for her, then she hugged Maryann and handed her the reins. The three of them walked Ali to the arena. Becky stood at the rail and watched as Aunt Ginny gave Maryann a boost up to mount. "He's quite a bit taller than Quesa, isn't he?" Maryann said in surprise. Ginny smiled.

"Yes he is, but you never rode him before so you probably didn't notice the difference."

Maryann walked him around and let him loosen up before she asked him to collect and trot. He felt a lot like Quesa but she also noticed he had more power in his movements. As she walked him past Becky, she whispered, "Boy, this is like Quesa on steroids!"

Becky giggled. "Wait 'til you get him going!" she told her.

Maryann pushed Ali into a strong trot for a lap around the arena. She was ready to whoop out loud. "Golly, he's got so much horsepower under the skin. He's sure fun to ride!" She pulled him back to a normal trot because he was a little out of shape. She kept him going for several laps in both directions. "Should I go ahead and canter?" she asked Aunt Ginny.

Ginny nodded. "We'll just do a couple of laps, then give him a rest and walk him out. He's starting to sweat already."

Maryann's ride was short but sweet. Prince Ali's canter was smooth as glass. His trot was easy to post. His strong trot was exciting. She understood why Becky wanted to ride him. Ali seemed to enjoy himself through every change of gait. But, by the time Ginny called the ride to a halt, Ali was sweating quite a bit. "He's out of shape. He needs short rides until he gets back into shape," she announced. "Becky, can you ask someone to start lounging him every day? That will improve his stamina a lot. Maryann will be able to ride a little longer each time we come and he should be ready for you to start your own practice on him."

Becky agreed. She and Maryann put Ali back in cross ties and removed the tack. They took him to the indoor wash rack and bathed him. Maryann put him on the hot walker to let him stretch his legs while he dried off. The girls brushed him down and put him back in his stall. Maryann gave him some apple pieces she'd brought with her. The two girls chatted happily as they worked.

"Why don't you stay for dinner here before you head back up the hill, Aunt Ginny? You remember what a good cook Esperanza is. She made extra hoping you'd stay. She told me she missed you," Becky said.

"I'd love to!" Ginny said. "But we need to check in with Maryann's mom and I have to call home first. Mike and Brody will be on their own for dinner. That means Mike will go out for pizzas or hamburgers. That won't break Brody's heart." She laughed.

Becky's mom, Caroline, joined everyone on the back patio by the pool when they finished up in the barn. Caroline invited Ginny to have an iced tea with her. Becky took Maryann to her room so she could show her pictures of Ali in the show ring. As they walked down the hallway to Becky's bedroom, Maryann got a glance into the living room. She was amazed. The entire house she lived in would fit into that one room here. When they got to Becky's bedroom, she thought most of her house would fit into that room too. She was astonished. Becky noticed her expression and her open mouth. "It's just a house, Maryann. My dad is an architect. He makes a lot of money. Don't let it scare you."

Maryann laughed nervously. "Oh, it didn't scare me. It's just funny, I guess. My whole house would fit into your living room. I've never seen a house this big before. It sure is beautiful."

"My mom says the most important thing is not where you live or how fancy your house is, it is what kind of person you are that counts," Becky told her. "She says you should be kind to everyone, give what you can to someone who has less than you, and try to be the best person you can be."

"Your mom and my mom will get along really well," Maryann told her. "She says the same thing!"

Before Esperanza, the housekeeper called them to dinner, Becky and Maryann talked about horses and horse shows. Becky told her all about the craziness that happened to her and Prince Ali. Becky also told her about going to the National Championships with Ali and her trip to Paris for the World Championships. Maryann was transported. She wanted nothing more than to take La Duquesa to the Youth National Championship in July with Becky and Ali. She just couldn't bring herself to ask her mom about it. She knew they couldn't afford it.

Becky called Aunt Ginny the next evening. They talked about Maryann. Becky wanted to know if there was any way she could help make sure La Duquesa become Maryann's for real and for certain. Ginny asked her to give it some time. Something would come up.

Ginny had a glimmer of an idea. If Maryann's grandparents disowned Rose before she knew she was pregnant with Maryann, maybe they didn't know they had a grandchild. If their son was really their only child, maybe they would be receptive to their only grandchild. And, if they were really wealthy, maybe they would be willing to help. She asked Brody to find out what Maryann's grandparents names were on the sly. She didn't want Maryann to know she was snooping around in her background.

Brody told her what Maryann knew about them the next evening while he helped her wash up dinner dishes. She had a name. Carnegie! That was an important east-coast family and if they were related to the Andrew Carnegie side, they could be more than rich. They could be filthy rich and famous too.

Ginny took some pictures of Maryann and La Duquesa the next day while they were riding in the arena. That night she started looking for Charles and Celeste Carnegie on the internet. She found them easily. Celeste was heavily involved

Chapter Ten

in charity work that extended from the east to west coast, raising money for children's charities and cancer research. She found a photo of the couple at a charity function printed in a major east coast newspaper. They were a handsome couple. Charles, a distinguished neurosurgeon at the best hospital in the east, had neatly groomed silver gray hair and looked handsome wearing a tuxedo in the picture. Celeste, looking years younger than her age, wore a fashionable gown and was dripping with jewels. They were what Ginny expected, and she noticed the resemblance Maryann had to her grandfather right away.

It took Ginny a day or two to make up her mind. She finally decided to go ahead with her plan. She wrote a letter to the Carnegies and included a close up picture of Maryann riding La Duquesa. She slipped it in the mail the next day and crossed her fingers. The letter would either bring her grandparents into Maryann's life or make no difference in her life if they rejected her. She prayed she'd made the right decision and the grandparents would welcome their only grandchild.

67

CHAPTER ELEVEN

Maryann and Aunt Ginny spent two days a week driving to San Juan Capistrano so Maryann could ride Prince Ali. Becky asked her mother or Luis, their barn supervisor, to lounge Ali every day. Between the riding and the lounging, his condition improved a lot in a short time. He was almost fit to ride in a show.

Maryann rode La Duquesa at Ginny's ranch as often as she could. She still took her lessons with Melissa, Susie, Kathy and Heidi on Wednesdays. The five girls worked hard and played hard afterwards, sometimes taking short trail rides before finishing up for the day. Since most of them planned to attend Youth Nationals in July, lessons were on Saturday mornings as well. Saturday afternoon was in San Juan Capistrano with Prince Ali, so Maryann had very little time for anything else. She was looking forward to school ending for the summer so she could spend more time riding.

***

Celeste Carnegie was in her office working on one of her numerous charity events when the butler brought her the mail for the day. She held the stack of envelopes in one hand and flipped through them, pulling a few aside that related to the project she was working on. A single envelope jumped out at her. It was a plain envelope, not one of the fancy engraved ones she normally got from donors, friends and other supporters. It had a return address from a Virginia Hartley with a post office box number in Pinon Hills, California. Celeste knew where Beverly Hills, California was and had visited friends there. Pinon Hills was a mystery to her. She had no idea where that was, nor was Virginia Hartley a name familiar to her. She had a lot to get done that day so she put the envelope aside for later and went on with her project.

Celeste came across that envelope again several days later. She picked it up and looked at it one more time. She was about to toss it in the trash can under her desk and decided to open it instead. Curiosity got the best of her. When she pulled out the letter, a photograph fell face-down on her desk. She read the letter. By the time she was done reading it, tears streaked down her face. She picked up the photograph and turned it over. She broke down completely. She sobbed as if her heart was broken. The maid heard her from another room and came running to see what was wrong. Celeste couldn't speak. She just kept sobbing and staring at the photograph.

Alarmed, the maid rushed downstairs to find Charles. He had guests at the time. She pulled him aside and told him there was something terribly wrong and he needed to get upstairs to his wife's office right away. Charles excused himself and rushed upstairs. He found Celeste sobbing. She was unable to tell him anything but she handed him the letter. Standing, he read what Virginia Hartley had to say then almost fell into the chair behind him. Celeste handed him the photograph that came with the letter. It took his breath away. He was staring at a feminine version of his own son! They knew! There was no doubt in their minds!

Charles got up from the chair and walked around Celeste's desk, pulling her to her feet and wrapping his arms around her. He held her until she calmed down. They sat back down and stared at each other for a few minutes. "What do you want to do about this?" he finally asked her.

"How soon can we fly to California?" she asked.

"How about day after tomorrow," he said. "I need a day to clear my schedule and I'm sure you do too. Why don't you make flight arrangements and clear your schedule. I'll get rid of my company downstairs and start clearing mine. What do you think we need? A week?"

"What if she doesn't want to see us?" Celeste almost whispered.

"We'll have to cross that bridge when we get to it," Charles answered gently. "Let's go and hope for the best. We have a lot of apologizing to do when we get there."

Celeste took a deep breath and exhaled slowly. "You're right about that. Me especially. We lost our son almost 14 years ago. That also cost us 13 years with our only grandchild.

I was so hateful that night. I said horrible things to her. I've thought about it many times. She didn't deserve it but I had no idea how to reach her and apologize. I was hurting so badly I just wanted to hurt something else and she became my target. I've done a lot of thinking over the years. If we could go back, I would change a lot of things. You remember Chip growing up. He always had a pencil and sketch pad in his hands when he wasn't playing sports or riding his polo ponies. WE decided he had to go into medicine. That's why he was away at college in the first place. And I decided I was better equipped to pick a wife for him. That's why I rejected

Rose. She didn't fit MY standards. If I had let him make up his own mind, he would be here with us right now."

"Don't beat yourself up now," Charles said quietly. "We can't go back, but we may be able to go forward. Let's get ourselves ready and make the trip. Maybe, just maybe, we can salvage a beautiful granddaughter out of this mess. I will call that Virginia Hartley and let her know we're coming. I'd like to surprise Maryann if we can."

Celeste had more trouble planning her wardrobe for this trip than she ever did before. She cleared her calendar for a week, claiming an emergency in the family. She made flight reservations to Ontario International Airport. She had no idea where that was. She booked them a suite at the local Hilton Hotel and set up a limousine to pick them up and drive them to Pinon Hills. She had no idea where that was either but it didn't matter. That was where her granddaughter lived.

Celeste flew all the time. She flew to Europe. She flew to the Far East. She flew to South America. She flew to Africa. She was nervous as they boarded the flight to Ontario. She could hardly contain herself. Charles had the jitters himself. They didn't know what kind of reception they would get when they landed. They desperately wanted the meeting to go well.

The limousine driver met them at their terminal when their flight landed and stowed their luggage in the trunk. He helped Mrs. Carnegie into the limousine. He asked Charles, "Where to?" Charles gave him the address he'd gotten from Virginia Hartley. The limo driver was not familiar with the area and had to look it up on his GPS before they left. He told Charles it would take at least an hour to get there. Charles mixed them a drink from the limo bar and settled back for a long ride. Celeste hardly knew what to do with herself. She barely took a sip of her drink and stared out the window as the limousine traveled along the highway toward Las Vegas.

Ginny called Rose at the hardware store and told her she had some special guests arriving that afternoon she wanted her to meet. She told her they were going to watch Maryann ride La Duquesa.

Maryann arrived at the ranch and handled her chores first. She wanted to ride. Brody told her they were expecting guests but he didn't know who they were or why they were coming. Maryann finished up her chores and tacked up La Duquesa. She had just started riding when the limousine showed up at the gate. She'd never seen a limousine in this area before. It surprised her. She wondered who the fancy people were who got out of it and were talking with Aunt Ginny on the deck. Maryann concentrated on her riding and ignored them. Ginny walked the guests to the rail at the top of the arena. The three adults watched her ride for several passes before Aunt Ginny called her over.

"Maryann, these are some nice people I'd like you to meet," she said.

Celeste opened her mouth first. "My name is Celeste and this is my husband, Charles," she told her. "We've heard quite a lot about you and wanted to meet you."

Maryann looked at her fancy clothes puzzled. "Why would you want to meet me?" she asked.

"Actually, we wanted to meet you because you are our granddaughter," Celeste told her.

"No way! My mom's parents are dead," Maryann said looking at the woman strangely.

"We're not your mom's parents, honey. We are your father's parents," Celeste said gently as she could.

"The mean, rich ones?" Maryann exclaimed with her eyes open wide. She slapped her hand over her mouth. She couldn't believe that came out like that.

Charles grinned at her. "Yes, my dear that probably describes who we used to be."

Celeste piped in, "I was very mean to your mother once. I promise never to be mean to anyone again as long as I live."

Charles laughed. "We wanted to get to know you. You are our only grandchild and we didn't know about you until your friend here, Virginia, contacted us. Would you be willing to give us another chance?"

"I guess so, as long as mom doesn't mind," Maryann answered uncertainly.

"I understand your mom is coming here soon and we'll talk to her then. In the meantime, who is that beautiful horse you are riding? I've never seen one so lovely. You know your father used to ride polo ponies but nothing as beautiful as that one," Charles told her.

"Really? My dad used to ride horses? I guess that shouldn't surprise me. I don't know much about him. Mom doesn't say much. Maybe you can tell me more about my dad?"

"Oh, we'd be delighted to tell you all about your dad. You look so much like him, you know," Celeste answered.

"Well, if you don't mind, I only have a few more minutes of practice time with Quesa. I'd like to finish my ride, then maybe we can talk some more in the barn while I groom her and put her away," Maryann suggested. She was trying to wrap her mind around these visitors and needed some time with her horse alone. Grandparents! Who'd have thought? And they didn't seem to be mean at all. She needed to adjust. She didn't know what her mother would say.

"Do you mind if we just watch you?" Celeste asked.

"No, not at all, but you might want to stay back a little so you don't get dust all over your fancy clothes," Maryann answered. She continued her ride while her head whirled. Who were these people? She's heard so little about them from her mother. It would be nice to hear more about her dad.

CHAPTER TWELVE

S am Brown had that prickly feeling along the back of his neck when he left the Coroner's office. That usually raised red flags for him but he just didn't get it. The coroner was convinced Reilly Stone was stone-dead before he fell down the steps in front of the cabin in Pinon Hills. If Sam remembered correctly, it would be hard to tell if there was a struggle of any kind at that cabin. The whole place was a mess. He called his friend Charlie. "Hey, Charlie! What are you doing for lunch tomorrow? Could you meet me at our favorite Denny's about 12:30? I've got an interesting case and just wanted to run some things past you."

Charlie Spade met Sam Brown often with either a case of his own or one of Sam's. They had been partners with the department years earlier and they'd worked well together. Sam missed working officially with him. They had a loose arrangement where they would get together off the record to discuss cases.

The next day, both men slid into a booth at the back of the restaurant the hostess led them to and took their menus from her, ordering coffees.

"How's the wife?" Charlie asked.

"Same as always. She's pushing me to retire soon. Maybe I can hook up with you and your practice then. I can't imagine staying home 24/7."

"Yeah, know what you mean. What did you want to talk to me about?" Charlie asked sipping his coffee.

"I have an interesting case that kind of raises red flags in my mind. I'd just like to give you my impressions of an interview I did and see what you think."

"Okay, shoot."

"I was called out on a death in Pinon Hills some time back. A kid out riding his dirt bike called it in to dispatch. He told the operator he'd seen a dead body around a cabin way out in the hills. He had to give the GPS coordinates to get us there. There was only one little road to that cabin and you could miss that if you weren't looking for it. The first deputy to arrive took the kid's statement and let him go. He went to the cabin and saw the man lying on the steps with his head just off the bottom step and his legs stretched to the top step. Over and above the smell of death, the man smelled like a brewery. He was definitely dead so I was called in on the case. I had a heck of a time finding the place."

"Sounds like he got drunk and fell to me," Charlie mused.

"That's what I thought when I got there too. The property around the cabin was littered with bottles, beer cans and trash so it looked like he'd been there a while. I had the photographer take pictures of the body as we found it. The door to the cabin was open so I had him take a couple of photos from the deck to the inside as well. The inside of that place was a complete mess with trash, bottles and cans everywhere. None of us went inside. Didn't appear we needed to."

"Okay, what happened next?"

"We called the coroner to pick up the body and I taped the cabin with crime scene tape and left. I had the guy's wallet in my evidence bag and looked up his next of kin for notification. I took a deputy with me and went to the address I found for the man's wife."

"Sounds pretty much by the book so far."

"When we got to the house, all the blinds were closed and the house looked like there was no one home. I rang the bell and saw out of the corner of my eye someone inside pulled the drapery back. She must have seen the Sheriff's car in the driveway. I knew there was someone inside so we waited. I had to ring the doorbell a second time to get any response. We heard the deadbolt unlocking and a door chain unhooking before the door opened a tiny crack. A woman asked us what we wanted. I told her we were looking for Anne Stone. She told us Anne Stone had passed away a couple of months earlier. I asked her who she was. She identified herself as Sara Evans, Anne Stone's niece. I asked her if we could come in to talk to her. She was very reluctant about letting us in. I think our badges must have been our ticket inside. She let us into her living room and sat opposite us in a chair while we sat on her sofa. I have to tell you that woman looked like a mouse with a cat on her tail. She was so nervous and jumpy."

"How did she react to the death notification?" Charlie asked.

"That was strange. When we got to that part, it was like letting the air out of an overfilled balloon. She just sank into that chair and deflated. It took her a minute or two before she finally sat up straight and got her wits about her again. She was an entirely different person. She answered our questions with complete sentences. I believe she was relieved. I'm thinking she was afraid of her uncle and his death released all that anxiety."

"How was she dressed when you saw her?" Charlie asked.

"That was strange too," Sam commented. "She was wearing a high turtle neck sweater and long pants in 80 degree weather. She also wore dark glasses the entire time we were in her house. That bothered me at the time. She turned her head once and I thought I could see a bruise on her left cheek. She kept her sleeves down to her wrists. I'm used to my wife wearing short sleeves or no sleeves at all when it's hot like that outside. That house was cold inside like the air conditioning was on full blast. But I have to tell you, that place was neat as a pin. I didn't see a speck of dust on the furniture or the hardwood floors anywhere. It was just strange the way the house was buttoned up and closed up so tight. It seemed to me she was afraid of something or someone, maybe Reilly Stone, until we told her he was dead."

"She had my phone number and gave me a call, probably the same day you were there," Charlie told him. "She said you referred her to me. She made an appointment for the next day, which would be the day after you visited her."

"Ah, yes, she said she needed a private investigator to help her locate her aunt's horse. She told me she spoke with her uncle and he told her he sold the horse. She also told me the horse had been given to her along with her aunt's home in her aunt's will."

"She brought the will to my office and I've looked it over. Sara Evans inherited everything her aunt had at the time of her death. She left nothing to her estranged husband, Reilly Stone, at all. And there was a considerable amount of money and property included in that will. Sara Evans will never have to work again, that's for sure."

"Really?" Sam replied. "Is the money a clue in this case?"

"If there is something hinky about Reilly Stone's death, there was a lot of money on the table. Sara Evans is a very rich woman. Her aunt was the Director of Equine Studies at Cal Poly Pomona when she died. She'd been a professor there for more than 30 years. She had a sizeable retirement account and she'd made some very prudent investments over the years. She wasn't the spendy type according to her niece. She invested money instead. Anne Stone was the sole heir to her parents' fortune. Most of that came as a complete surprise to Sara who had no idea her aunt was a multi-millionaire until the will was read by her aunt's attorney. She told me she was dumbfounded."

"How did Sara Evans appear to you during your interview?" Sam asked him.

"Must have been wearing the same clothes she wore the day before when you saw her. She was dressed in a high turtle neck sweater and long pants in 80+ degree weather, and she had on a pair of dark glasses the whole time she was in my office. I did see some ugly bruises on her arm she covered up quickly. She explained she dropped a heavy box while she was packing up some of her aunt's things. I also thought I saw a bruise on her cheek that she hadn't quite covered with make-up."

"How was her demeanor with you?" Sam questioned.

"She was a lot more relaxed than the Sara Evans you described when you first saw her. She brought in the will and showed me the information on the horse. She told me her aunt loved that horse to distraction and it was the first horse she'd ever owned. That sounded a little odd from a professor of equine studies. Sara said her aunt always told her she loved horses, but didn't want to own one because of the expense. Sara really thought her aunt lived exclusively on her own salary and was careful with money. I believe she was telling the truth there. She's still overwhelmed about her inheritance. I got the impression Sara Evans is a really nice young lady who genuinely loved her aunt. She quit her job to care for her when she was diagnosed with cancer. She used her own money getting her to and from doctor appointments and buying food for them. She bought some things for the cabin when her aunt suggested they move there and bring the horse. Sara told me Anne Stone wanted to be able to see the horse every day and that was the only place she could do that."

"Okay, so you think she is truthful?" Sam asked.

"I think she told me the truth and she told you the truth. But I think there might be a few things she is not talking about at all. She's not lying about it, just not telling us all that she knows," Charlie said. "I think there may be a little more to the story."

"Well, let me tell you one more little tidbit about this case," Sam said. "Reilly Stone did not fall down the steps at the cabin and break his neck and die. His cause of death was blunt force trauma to the left side of his head! How about those apples? He was dead before his neck snapped on the steps."

"Are you kidding me?" Charlie asked. "Is that what the coroner told you?"

"Sure is." Sam answered between bites of his sandwich. "The coroner didn't get around to Reilly Stone for weeks because his case looked like a cut-and-dry accidental death. When he did get started on the autopsy, somethings looked strange to him so he took a few more x-rays. He found a deep depressed skull fracture on his left temple that was the real cause of death. He was already dead before he collapsed on the stairs. The broken neck happened after that."

"Any idea what caused the injury?" Charlie asked in surprise.

"Nope. The coroner said there was no trace evidence in the wound but it looked like something large and flat hit him on the side of his head. The blow sent bone shards deep into his brain, killing him instantly."

"Is he reclassifying the case from accidental death to homicide?" Charlie wondered.

"Looks like it at the moment. I've been working on this case for a while and getting nowhere. This is about all I know about the guy. He drove a new model Mercedes sedan. I went through the car myself. I found several 36-packs of beer and several bottles of cheap scotch in the trunk. I found the receipt on the passenger seat along with a high-end bottle of scotch he'd already opened and drank part of, maybe on his way home? The receipt was dated a week before we found the body, probably the day he died. Apparently he hadn't had time to bring the "groceries" inside before someone whacked him. And there was $350.00 in his wallet plus some change in the car. Driver's license and auto insurance card in the wallet but no credit cards, no photos, nothing else. The only other thing in the car was a nice set of golf clubs."

"Wow! A new Mercedes sedan? Those are pricey for someone living like a drunk hermit in a cabin in the woods." Charlie exclaimed.

"Yeah, I called the dealership and talked to the manager there. He told me Reilly Stone called a new order in every year. Always a new sedan with all the bells and whistles. He brings in a deposit of $20,000 in cash, like hundred dollar bills in a suitcase, and waits for his new car. When the car arrives the manager calls his cell phone and gives him the total. He brings it in a suitcase in hundred dollar bills, pays tax, license fees, takes his keys and they don't see him again until the next year. They don't have an address for him, just the cell phone number."

"So do you know what he does for a living? He has to have a job that pays pretty well to afford a new Mercedes every year." Charlie asked.

"We can't find anything on him. He had no visible means of support, no job, no social security payments, no nothing!" Sam told him. "He's a real mystery."

"Tell you what; I have some time on my hands. Why don't you forward over what you have on him and this case and I'll put in some time and see what I can dig up. Give me the cell phone number. I have a friend who can help me run his calls down. I'm really curious about this one. Let's keep in touch and share what we find out. Maybe two heads are better than one," Charlie suggested.

"Sounds good to me," Sam agreed.

CHAPTER THIRTEEN

Rose was surprised when she arrived at Hartley Ranch to pick up Maryann and saw a black stretch limousine in the driveway. Nobody rode around these dirt roads in one of those. She was curious as she parked and walked toward the barn. She could see La Duquesa in cross ties and her daughter doing something with her. Ginny was also there with a couple of people she didn't recognize at first. Ginny called her earlier in the day and told her they were having some visitors at the ranch so she was curious about them.

As she got closer to the barn she could see an older couple talking to Maryann and Ginny. She didn't recognize them until she stepped into the barn. When she did recognize them, she wished she could just disappear.

Maryann was the first one to speak to her. "Hey, Mom. Guess who these nice people are?"

"I know who they are, sweetheart," she answered woodenly. "I'm just wondering what they are doing here?"

Celeste walked up to Rose and offered her hand. Rose just stood there staring at her. Celeste dropped her hand and took a deep breath, "Rose, I know what a horrible person I was to you. I remember all the terrible things I said to you that night. I have no excuse for that. We came out here to see you and apologize for it and hope you can find it in your heart to forgive me."

Charles walked over and stood beside his wife. "We didn't know about Maryann until your friend, Virginia, wrote us and sent a picture of her. She looks just like Chip did when he was her age. There's no doubt in our minds that Maryann is our granddaughter. We'd like to earn your forgiveness and get to know your daughter, our granddaughter, if you will permit it."

Rose was staggered by this development. She had to find a bench to sit down on before she fell. Her knees and legs wouldn't support her. "How do you feel about all this, Maryann?" Rose asked her daughter.

"Well, Mom, it would be kind of nice to find out more about my dad. And Mr. and Mrs. Carnegie seem nice enough. What do you think?" Maryann said, embarrassed her mother asked her such a personal question in public.

"If that's what you want, I will agree to it," Rose said thoughtfully. "If you are ever uncomfortable, please come tell me."

Celeste and Charles Carnegie stood listening to this exchange with their hearts in their throats. They wanted Rose to say yes. They wanted to get to know their granddaughter. They wanted her to love them as much as they loved her already. They sighed with relief when Rose said she would agree to let them see Maryann.

"Can we start off by asking you two to dinner?" Charles asked. "And, Rose, we have some things to discuss with you if that's okay with you."

"At this hour, Aunt Adele probably already has dinner started," Rose began. "I can't just walk out on her and Uncle Roy that way."

"Well, just a suggestion mind you, but why don't you call them now and ask them if they would care to join us?" Charles offered.

Rose made the call. Aunt Adele and Uncle Roy were just as mystified as she was with this development. They wanted to meet the Carnegies too. But they were lukewarm in their feelings about them after what they'd put Rose through all those years ago.

Despite all their pretty words to her, Rose was lukewarm about them as well. She didn't want to get hurt like that again, ever again. And she didn't want her little girl hurt by them either so she went along cautiously.

Rose took Maryann home when she finished up with La Duquesa. Charles asked the limousine driver to follow her. That way everyone could pile in the limousine for the drive to the restaurant for dinner. Charles would have them dropped off at home before he and Celeste went back to their hotel for the night.

The Carnegies left the choice of restaurant up to Rose. They didn't know the area at all. Rose chose a restaurant she could never afford herself but one that came recommended by friends who could. The restaurant had nice seating for the family and had a reputation for excellent food.

Celeste locked onto Maryann and made sure she was seated beside her. She spent the entire meal talking with Maryann about her school, her grades, her interests, and about that beautiful horse she was riding when they first saw her. She wanted to know everything about her granddaughter. Maryann, on the other hand, had a million questions about her dad. So Celeste and Maryann spent the entire time in their own conversation and barely heard anyone else.

Charles needed to talk to Rose. He told her he needed her and Maryann's full legal names and their social security numbers if possible. Rose looked at him like he had suddenly grown another head on his shoulders. He laughed. "Guess I should have prefaced that with a reason. My lawyer needs that information for some work I'm having him do right now. The truth is you and Maryann are our only legal heirs. We're having our wills redone now so that you and your daughter are named in them as they should be. Also, Chip had his own trust account when he died. I didn't have the heart to change it but I did oversee it and made some good investments with the funds. They've grown exponentially in the last 14 years. We'd like to grant that trust fund to your daughter with you as trustee until she reaches age 21 if that's agreeable with you. But the caveat is that we get to help teach her the value of money so she will know how to handle it when that time comes. Just in small doses, you see. We don't want to scare her or anything."

"Out of curiosity, just how much is in that trust fund?" Rose asked, not sure she really wanted to know yet.

Charles gave her a number that she could hardly comprehend. She asked him to repeat it and still couldn't wrap her mind around it. How many zeros was that? She lost count. She couldn't respond. She just sat there with a silly blank stare until Charles patted her arm. "It's okay young lady. It's a lot to take in on short notice. But we do have some suggestions for using some of the money. First, I'd like to see you get a home of your own on enough land to put up an equestrian facility for Maryann, you know, a barn, an arena, a tack room and all the goodies."

"I can't do that. I can't leave Uncle Roy and Aunt Adele alone. They took me in when I really needed help. They're getting up in years and are going to need my help soon enough."

Celeste caught part of the conversation between Charles and Rose. She patted Rose's arm and said, "Buy a bigger house, dear! You can afford it," and turned her attention back to Maryann as if that problem was solved so easily.

Charles continued, "I'd also like to see you get better transportation. I hear from Uncle Roy he spends most of his time under the hood of one or the other vehicle you have and the rest of his time coming up with band aids for the next breakdown. You can certainly afford new vehicles so we don't have to worry about any of you driving out here in the country in a car that's apt to break down any minute. We worry about the safety of all four of you."

Rose didn't remember much else of the conversation that evening. Her head was swimming. She didn't want to be bought by anyone and wasn't absolutely sure that's not what the Carnegies were doing. She hoped not for Maryann's sake, but she wasn't ready to completely trust them. She decided to take it one day at a time and see what happened next. She was happy to step back inside the home she shared with Aunt Adele and Uncle Roy. It was safe. It was home. She felt the love that radiated there. She put her daughter to bed and had a long soak in the tub before she too went to bed for the night.

CHAPTER FOURTEEN

C harlie Spade found some answers in the mail. There was an envelope from the Arabian Horse Registry in Denver, Colorado on his desk. He opened the large envelope and read through the letter and reviewed the paperwork attached. La Duquesa has been re-registered to a Virginia Hartley in Pinon Hills about two weeks after Reilly Stone's death. Virginia Hartley had her mail addressed to a post office box, so he didn't have a location for her. The registry didn't have a phone number either. Well, he was a private investigator and that's what they do. They find people.

Charlie looked for the largest feed store in Pinon Hills figuring if Virginia Hartley had a horse, she would need supplies. There wasn't one. He did find two listed in the adjacent little town of Phelan and called them. The first one didn't recognize her name. The second one did. The manager said, "Oh, you must mean Ginny. She and her husband own Hartley Ranch in Pinon Hills. They buy a lot of feed from us." The woman was happy to give Charlie an address when he told her he wanted to talk with Ginny about a horse. She also gave him directions because she told him Google Maps weren't always trustworthy out in their area. Charlie checked his schedule for that afternoon and decided to take a drive out to meet Ginny Hartley. He packed up his paperwork, grabbed his cell phone and told his secretary he'd be gone for the balance of the day.

Charlie drove the hour and ten minutes to the front gate of Hartley Ranch. It was no small ranch for certain. The house was a few steps from the walk-through gate. It was a large Spanish style hacienda with covered porch along the entire front and large partially covered patio at the rear. "Horses must be good business," he thought as he walked to the door and rang the bell. He heard the dog alarm go off inside and fade a bit as the dog made his way to the back of the house. He heard someone shushing the dog as they walked to the front door. An older woman answered the door. "Hello, what can I do for you?" she asked pleasantly.

"I'm here to talk to a Virginia Hartley about a horse," he answered smiling.

"Well if you came to talk about a horse, you came to the right place. Come on in. We can talk in the living room." She ushered him in and told the dog, Clyde, to go back outside and leave them alone. "Clyde can be a pest sometimes," she explained. "He's friendly but a nuisance."

She escorted Charlie to the living room and offered him a seat. "Now what exactly are you looking for. My husband has several really nice Quarter horses and a lovely Paint mare that are ready for competition if that's your preference. I know he also has some ready to be trail horses if you like to ride for relaxation."

"Actually, I came here to talk to you about a specific Arabian horse. I have some documentation here I'd like to show you. First is a copy of her registration papers showing you as her owner. Second is a copy of Anne Stone's will leaving the horse to her niece, Sara Evans, upon her death." He handed the papers to Ginny.

Ginny looked at the registration papers and was stunned to see La Duquesa's name. "Wait a minute here. Just exactly what are you doing here?" she asked him with an edge in her voice.

"I'm Charlie Spade, a private investigator. I was hired by Sara Evans to find her property. She was Anne Stone's only heir and she died a few months ago. Sara thought the horse went back to Anne Stone's trainer the day she passed away. She told me she called her before she left her aunt's cabin in Pinon Hills and asked her to pick the horse up for her while Sara took care of funeral arrangements and some of her aunt's other business. When she talked to the trainer just a couple of weeks ago, the trainer said the gentleman who was living in the cabin drove her off and told her the horse belonged to him. Sara had a conversation with the gentleman, who was Anne Stone's estranged husband, and he told Sara he sold the horse. But, as you can see from the will in your hand, he had no right to sell her to anyone at all. The horse belongs to Sara Evans."

Ginny looked at the will and read it carefully. It was in black and white. Anne Stone gave La Duquesa to Sara Evans when she died. Ginny's heart sank.

"Well, Charlie, let me tell you a few things. Anne Stone was one of my professors when I was in the equine studies section at Cal Poly Pomona years back. She was my favorite professor. I've remained loosely in touch with Anne since. We didn't see each other often, but called each other once in a while to catch up. My husband also had her in one of his classes. That's where I met him. I was at Anne's funeral myself. I met Sara Evans at the funeral. In all the years I knew Anne Stone, I never knew her to own a horse. She always told me they were an expensive hobby she couldn't afford on a professor's salary. But she had access to every one of the lovely Arabian horses born, raised and trained at Cal Poly and that was enough for her. This registration paperwork shocks me in the first place." Ginny got up and walked around the room with her hands clutched behind her back. Finally she told him she had something in her office she wanted him to see and left the room.

When she returned to the living room she handed him four photographs. They were pictures taken of La Duquesa the day she arrived at Hartley Ranch.

"My husband and I took a trail ride that Sunday morning with Clyde, our dog. You just met him. We were minding our own business when something alerted Clyde and he took off running. We chased him on horseback until we came to a cabin way out in a little valley we'd never seen before. There was an old drunk beating this horse with a lounge whip. That got Clyde's attention and he was charging the man when we got there. The man was trying to use the whip on our dog by then. My husband is particularly upset by any kind of horse abuse and that clearly was the case right there. That mare had maybe a week left before she died of starvation, thirst and exposure. I offered him cash to buy the mare. I happened to have feed money in my pocket that I'd forgotten to leave at the ranch before we went riding. I counted out $500 in his hand and he handed me her registration papers. He told me the horse was my problem and he slammed the door in my face. We took those pictures when we got her back here. I wasn't sure we could save her life at that point."

"Oh, my goodness. That poor horse. I'm so sorry," Charlie said as he glanced at the photos again.

"To bring you up to date, with the help of our vet we were able to save her life. She's doing just fine now. I have a young student who can't afford the expense of a horse that has fallen in love with her. She works here to work off the cost of riding lessons. She's out in the arena riding La Duquesa right now. Why don't you come out and see her for yourself."

Ginny escorted Charlie out the back door to the riding arena. Maryann and La Duquesa were practicing. Charlie watched with interest. "Is that the same horse that's in those pictures you showed me?" he asked dumbfounded.

"Yes, that's the same horse. This is what good animal husbandry, a good vet and the love of a little girl can accomplish in a few months' time," Ginny told him. "Despite whatever paperwork someone has, sometimes you just know when the right horse comes along for the right person. You are looking at that in front of you now."

"Wow! Mrs. Hartley I don't know what to say. I'll tell you that I don't think Sara Evans is especially interested in the horse for herself. She didn't want her uncle anywhere near it and she sees it as a valuable asset her aunt gave her when she died. Let me talk to her. I think you are right. The horse is happy and healthy which were her major concerns. I think the horse is right where she belongs."

He turned to go and Ginny walked back toward the house with him. "Why don't you give me your phone number and I'll keep in touch with you on this," Charlie suggested. "Maybe we can work something out."

"Oh please try hard," Ginny asked. "The wrong decision will break two loving hearts."

CHAPTER FIFTEEN

The Carnegies were thrilled. Their granddaughter was a feminine version of their son in so many respects. She was reserved the way Chip was around strangers as a young teenager. Celeste found out she loved to draw and paint like her son and she had a deep love of horses the way he did. She never had the same advantages he did and was naive in a sweet way Celeste thought was adorable. "I'm so glad Ginny wrote us. If she hadn't we'd probably go to our graves not knowing what a beautiful grandchild we had," Celeste said. Charles nodded his agreement.

"I know Rose is suspicious of our motives. Why don't we stay a while? Maybe we can convince her that our intentions are good," suggested Charles.

They looked for a place to stay closer than the drive to and from the hotel in Ontario. Charles rented a new SUV so they didn't need a limousine to get them around. They called home and made arrangements for paperwork to be sent to them overnight as needed. Their cell phones would keep them in touch with anyone back home that required their attention. They settled in for the long run. They didn't want to leave until they'd won the hearts and minds of their new family.

Charles and Celeste showed up at Hartley Ranch to watch Maryann ride and spend time with her. Charles followed her around while she did her chores and helped where he could. He watched her clean one of the outside paddocks one day and stepped in to give her a hand. "Grandpa, you're going to mess up your shoes doing this!" Maryann told him.

He laughed. "Well, how else am I going to get to know you? If you are doing this, I certainly don't mind helping."

She pointed out the gunk stuck all over his custom-made shoes. "That's what I mean, Grandpa. You need to buy yourself some proper ranch clothes. Look at the rest of us. We wear jeans, shirts and boots we don't care about getting all messy. Your fancy clothes will get so smelly and dirty you'll never be able to wear them again. Grandma too! Those heels she wears are going to break her neck if she doesn't watch out. They're no good on a ranch."

Charles really didn't care about his clothes but he did take her advice. While she was at school the next day, he and Celeste went shopping. They came home with "proper ranch clothes" according to their granddaughter. Both showed up at the ranch later in jeans, plain shirts and paddock boots fresh from the local farm and ranch supply Ginny told them about. They'd even bought new cowboy hats to keep the sun off their faces. Maryann hardly recognized them when she got there.

"Whoa! Look at you guys! You look like ranchers now. That's more like it!" she told them. "Now, Grandpa, let's go get dirty!" The two laughed as they hurried off to do Maryann's chores leaving Celeste sitting on the deck talking with Ginny.

"How exactly did you get to know about Maryann?" she asked Ginny.

Ginny told her about Maryann's essay and the picture she'd drawn. She told her about her first conversation with Rose and her "we don't need charity" comment. She told her about Maryann's first visit to the ranch and how she looked when she first got to touch and smell a real horse. She told her about Maryann sitting under the feeder in the stall reading to La Duquesa and how that helped bring that dirty, skinny, scared out of her mind horse around to the horse she was today. "She's a remarkable young lady in so many ways," Ginny said.

When the chores were finished and Maryann was riding La Duquesa in the arena, Charles and Celeste sat with Ginny on the patio watching her. "I don't have much work to do with her now. She's a natural rider and intuitively knows how to handle herself with that horse," she told them. "All I do now is watch and offer suggestions when they are done riding."

Ginny thought about her conversation with Charlie Spade. She had no idea how long she would be able to keep La Duquesa. It was obvious there was someone else with a stronger claim on the horse than she had. She'd invested $500 and the cost of care and feeding. Maryann invested the love and work that helped bring La Duquesa back to the horse she was. There was no price tag you can put on love like that. She hoped to hear from Mr. Spade that there was something Ginny could do to keep the mare. She thought about that all the time now. She just kept it to herself.

Charles and Celeste rode with Ginny and Maryann to San Juan Capistrano the next time Maryann rode Prince Ali for Becky Howard. They were delighted with the big silver stallion and his owner. Becky was doing well and thought her doctor would finally release her to ride. She and Maryann were scheming about how they could get together with Prince Ali and La Duquesa to ride at the same time.

"Maybe we can talk Ginny into bringing La Duquesa here so you and I can practice our ring strategy together," Becky suggested. "That was what she and I were working on before I got hurt. It would be more fun with two of us riding together."

"What is ring strategy anyway?" Maryann asked.

"I know you've been taking lessons so I know you've heard Aunt Ginny tell you about entering the arena at a bold trot, smiling so you can make a great first impression on the judge. And she's probably talked about how to prevent another rider from covering you up so the judge doesn't see you on the rail in the class, right?"

Maryann nodded thoughtfully.

"Well, that's the stuff we need to be perfect with at Youth Nationals, silly girl!" Becky told her. "When we have a championship ride, it has to be perfect!"

"I don't even know if I'm going to Nationals this year," Maryann admitted. "I haven't talked to my mom about it because I don't think we can afford the cost of the whole thing. We'd have to be in Albuquerque for more than a week and stay in a hotel. We have to eat too, not just the horses. And I don't have an outfit for Country Pleasure classes. None of the other girls at the ranch ride that discipline so they don't have something I can borrow either." Maryann had been thinking about that for weeks now. She desperately wanted to go but didn't see how it would be possible. She cried herself to sleep more than once over it.

Rose had her own serious concerns. She didn't mention her conversation with Charles Carnegie over dinner. Maryann hadn't heard that, nor had Aunt Adele or Uncle Roy. The more she thought about it, the more concerned she was. Were their motives as pure as they presented them? Were they here to take her daughter away from her? Were they trying to buy her affection? Were they devious people who would do any of that? Rose kept her mouth shut and watched. If they were being underhanded, it would show up soon. Rose expected the other shoe to drop.

La Duquesa was concerned about a few things too. She often talked with Clyde in the barn and she heard about the strange man who visited Ginny. *"I didn't hear everything,"* Clyde told her, *"because Ginny sent me away. But he was a stranger in our house so I lay down in the hall so I could be close if Ginny needed me. That's my job. I protect my people."*

"What was he there for, anyway?" Quesa asked.

"He had a bunch of papers in his hand he showed to Ginny. He told her someone named Sara, I think, owns you because her aunt gave you to her when she died," Clyde relayed.

"Oh. No. I don't want to move again. I love it here. I love Ginny and I really love Maryann. I don't want to go away so I never get to see them again," Quesa whispered sadly.

"I don't think the issue is settled yet so don't get your hooves in a shake over it. The man saw the pictures of you when you first got here and Ginny took him outside and showed you to him while Maryann was riding you. I couldn't hear everything but I think he told Ginny maybe there was some way to work it out," Clyde said hopefully. *"Let's give the human's some time. Every once in a while they do the right thing, you know."*

"I know that. You helped them to help me or I wouldn't even be here right now. I just wish I knew I had a forever home with my one-and-only human and I wish with all my heart that could be Maryann."

CHAPTER SIXTEEN

B ecky called Aunt Ginny after school and relayed what
Maryann told her about the National Show. "Aunt
Ginny, she doesn't know if she can go to Nationals this year.
She doesn't think her mother can afford it. Is there anything
I can do to help her? I'd really like her to go with us. Of
course, that might depend on if my doctor says I can go, but
I'm going to work on him really, really hard," she giggled.
"Actually, I feel great and can't wait to ride Ali again. He'll
probably okay it when I see him next time. Mom bought me
a brand new Troxel helmet. I will take it with me to show
him my head will be protected."

"I guess I never thought how Maryann felt about going to
the Nationals with the rest of us. Guess I just assumed she
knew she was going along. Thanks for letting me know. Let
me work on it," Ginny told her. "You do what the doctor
says, young lady!"

"Yes, Auntie! Now you sound just like my
mother." Becky laughed.

When Ginny came up with the idea of taking Maryann
with the other girls to the big championship show, she

never talked about her plans with Maryann. Of course she would be paying all the entry fees and show fees and she would provide transportation for La Duquesa to and from Albuquerque, and she would feed Maryann the same way she would feed Brody. She just hadn't thought to pass the information on to Rose or Maryann. She would take care of that at the next opportunity.

Charles and Celeste picked Maryann up at school and brought her to the ranch to give Roy and Adele a break. It also gave them more time with their granddaughter. Celeste enjoyed sitting on the patio, sometimes with Ginny if she wasn't too busy, watching the activity on the ranch. Grandpa, as Charles was now referred to by Maryann, took off for the barn with her to get her chores started. They were cleaning water buckets today and scrubbing tack. Brody joined them with Clyde who always liked playing in the water. Once they finished cleaning buckets and getting well soaked in the process, Brody and Maryann sat Grandpa down on a stool in the tack room. They showed him the finer points of cleaning tack with saddle soap and finishing up with Neatsfoot oil. Grandpa was good with pulling bridles apart and cleaning the leather strips, but completely confused about how they went back together. Maryann patiently showed him what each part of the bridle was and how to put them back in the right place.

Grandpa looked at his clothes and mentioned besides the mud on his boots and jeans, he now had saddle soap on his shirt and had spilled Neatsfoot oil on his pants.

"Good!" Maryann told him. "Now you look like a rancher! Those new jeans were just too new. You need to get them good and dirty and wash them a few times. They get softer and more comfortable that way. Mine are the most comfortable just before mom decides to throw them out or

I outgrow 'em," she giggled. "We're going to make a rancher out of you yet!"

Brody added, "You really need a little horse poop on the boots too! Gives them the well-worn look you're looking for."

Grandpa had a good laugh. "Guess I need to get with the program here then. Give me some more Neatsfoot oil to spill and I'll be sure to walk through a stall or two before we leave."

Grandpa stayed in the barn after the tack was cleaned and put away and helped sweep out the tack room. Maryann got La Duquesa out of her stall and tacked her up for a practice ride. Brody decided to ride Bobbie with her. Grandpa had lots of questions about the different saddles and tack they used. Maryann and Brody were happy to teach him about what they used and what the purpose of each piece was. He was impressed by their knowledge and skills. When the horses were ready, Grandpa walked to the arena with them and stood with one foot on the lower rail, leaning on the top rail watching them.

Ginny came out of the house after finishing up some paperwork in her office and found Celeste sitting on the patio enjoying a convenience store iced tea. She joined her. "How's your day going," she asked her.

"This is absolutely wonderful. I've never been to this part of California before. We went to Palm Springs once for a golf event for Charles but I've never seen such a beautiful desert. You have so much green around with the junipers and the Joshua trees. The wildflowers are still blooming here and they are lovely. I understand you get snow in the winter here?"

"Yes, our Spring and early Summers are lovely. There is a lot more green to our desert than the lower desert around Palm Springs. We don't get the heat they do either, but we do get pretty cold in the winter. Part of that is because of our elevation. We are a little over 4,000 feet above sea level here. We do get some snow in the winter, but it doesn't stick around like it does for you folks on the East Coast or Midwest," Ginny told her.

The two women noticed Maryann and Brody riding into the arena and Charles, in his jeans, boots and cowboy hat leaning on the arena rail. Celeste grinned. "He's starting to look like an old cowhand isn't he?" She laughed. "Didn't take Maryann long to rub off on him."

Ginny grinned at the sight. "Speaking of Maryann, she told Becky she didn't think she could afford to go to the Championship Show in July. I guess I'd better talk to Rose. I'm paying the expenses so Rose doesn't have to worry. I can't wait to see what Maryann and La Duquesa do to the competition there. They are going to be the ones to beat in her division. I should know. I rode that division myself as a girl. It's tough, but Maryann and Quesa are tougher."

Celeste thought about what Ginny said. Obviously Rose hadn't told anyone about her conversation with Charles the other night. Charles received a packet from his lawyer that morning at the hotel. It included copies of their wills for signature and copies of the trust documents giving Maryann more than twenty-seven million dollars. Rose was listed as trustee on the account until Maryann turned 21. There was no reason for Ginny to pay the expenses. Maryann had plenty of money now, once the documents were signed. Celeste decided to leave things alone until she spoke with Charles. Rose had not refused the money, but she'd not accepted it either. Celeste didn't want to rock the boat.

When Charles walked up from the barn, Celeste pulled him aside and told him about the conversation with Ginny. "Oh, heck no! Ginny doesn't need to pay for our granddaughter," he said. "Let's go talk to her. I want to make sure Maryann has the best of everything. We can afford to pay for that. We need to talk to Rose in the next day or two about the trust account. I'm in agreement with you. Let's not rock that boat, but we can buy Maryann what she needs for the show ourselves."

Charles pulled Ginny aside. "I was talking with Maryann in the barn a few minutes ago. She told me she uses your tack for the shows because she only has a few pieces of her own. Rose, Adele and Roy have been shopping for her at used tack sales. I'd like to fix that and get her brand new stuff of her very own. Celeste and I have missed a lot of birthdays and Christmases in her life so we want to make some of that up. Can you help us with that?"

Ginny was surprised. "Well, sure. I'd be happy to help. What did you have in mind?"

"We want to give you the money to buy Maryann the finest saddle and tack available. From what I remember of Chip's equestrian involvement, the saddle alone will cost between $3,000 and $5,000 for the top of the line. She needs a bridle which could go for between $800 and $1200, leathers and stirrups, girth and saddle pad which would probably add another $1,000 to $2,000 to that. And she needs a good saddle cover and bridle bag. I talked to her about her show clothes. She told me she has been wearing some used items her mom found her and borrowing from the other girls but none of them ride her discipline now. She needs a Day coat, jodhpurs, boots, blouse, and derby. We'd like her to have two of everything and maybe three pairs of jods because we know kids and horses get them dirty quickly. We want the best tailoring, best fabrics and best style for her. That should add maybe another $5,000 to the cost. If I write you a check right now for $15,000 can you help get all of that and anything else you know she needs?"

This time Ginny was shocked. $15,000 to outfit one child? These people were serious! They weren't kidding! She swallowed hard, nodding her head. "Of course I will help. I need to get orders in right away for custom items and we'll need to have the Day coats and jods fitted by a tailor. We have enough time. I don't think it will take quite that much money though."

Charles looked at her seriously. "Top of the line, best available, nothing less will do for our baby girl. Spend it and let me know if you need more. Celeste and I are grateful for your help with this. We'd have no idea where to buy what she needs out here. Thank you so much."

Charles pulled the checkbook out of Celeste's purse and wrote the check on the spot. He handed it to Ginny and hugged her. "You have no idea how much this means to us."

CHAPTER SEVENTEEN

S ara Evans sat at her aunt's desk crying her eyes out. She'd just hung up the phone after a call from Charlie Spade. He told her what he'd found out about La Duquesa. He explained the horse was re-registered to Virginia Hartley in Pinon Hills. Her ranch was not far from the cabin she shared with her aunt during her aunt's final days. Apparently Aunt Annie had taken La Duquesa's registration papers with her when they moved to the cabin. That just pointed out again how much the mare meant to her aunt. She didn't know they were tucked in her aunt's belongings and had not gone back to the cabin to clean it out after the hospice people removed her aunt's body that morning. Reilly Stone must have found them. He'd given them to Mrs. Hartley when she bought La Duquesa from him, probably the morning before he died.

If she had only gone to the cabin sooner, maybe she could have prevented what Mr. Spade described as neglect and abuse that La Duquesa suffered at Reilly Stone's hand. La Duquesa meant so much to Aunt Annie and she had let them both down in a terrible way. The guilt tore at her heart. It took quite a while to get herself under control. She made a cup of tea and sat in Aunt Annie's living room staring at the photograph of La Duquesa, begging their forgiveness.

When she calmed down, her mind went back in time thinking about Aunt Annie. La Duquesa was the only horse she'd ever owned. Even though she was in charge of the Equine Studies programs at Cal Poly Pomona, Annie always said horses were too expensive for a woman on a professor's salary. Aunt Annie enjoyed all the beautiful Arabian horses at the campus without having to spend her own money taking care of them. Sara was completely taken aback when Aunt Annie called and told her she bought herself a horse. Conversations with Aunt Annie always centered on the horse from that moment forward. Annie was in love with La Duquesa. There was nothing about the horse that wasn't perfect, adorable, elegant, or loving as far as she was concerned. She'd even brought the mare to the campus on occasion so she could spend more time with her while she was working.

Sara was never interested in horses. She was in the cheer-squad in high school and dated athletes. She didn't have time for an outside interest that would take up so much of her spare time. Then came college. During her first year, she continued dating athletes for a while but they seemed to be interested in drinking and partying. She almost flunked a couple of classes. Aunt Annie took her aside and had a stern talk with her about her future. She stopped with all the freshman antics and got serious about her education. She had even less spare time for outside interests. With Aunt Annie's urging, she extended her education an additional two years and earned her Master's Degree. She interned with a public agency to pay her bills and they happily took her on as a full-time employee when she finished school. She thought about it. She still didn't have a lot of spare time for outside interests but maybe that was just her choice. She'd seen others that did.

Sara's parents passed away before she finished her freshman year of college. She'd managed to finish her education with some help from Aunt Annie, part time jobs and a lot of student loans. She's paid on those loans until Anne Stone's death. Her aunt left her more than enough to pay them off so she really didn't need to work. She had time on her hands. Should she try to spend time with La Duquesa now? Was that what she wanted? She had no idea. The tea cup in her hand began to shake. She set it down in the saucer. What did SHE want now?

If she took La Duquesa back, she would have to put her with a trainer. She lived in Aunt Annie's home in a suburban neighborhood. She couldn't keep a horse there. And she had no idea how to ride a horse or take care of one. She would have to take lessons and learn a lot about horses quickly to do justice to her aunt's "heart-horse."

Tears leaked out of her eyes again when she thought about what Mr. Spade told her. Virginia Hartley showed him photographs of La Duquesa the day she picked her up at the cabin. Her Aunt and La Duquesa deserved better than that. She felt responsible for it. She made one quick phone call that morning and simply forgot about the horse for over two months. How could she do that? Maybe she wasn't the one who should be responsible for the horse again. She failed miserably the first time.

She thought about the young Maryann Wilcox. Mr. Spade told her the girl had been responsible for much of La Duquesa's rehabilitation and the mare was very fond of the girl. He told her what Virginia Hartley told him about their relationship. The girl was crazy about La Duquesa.

Sara thought about herself at that age and a few years older. She was so concerned about wearing the right outfit and having perfect hair and make-up that she'd forget her homework if Mom didn't remind her to take it to school. Would Maryann be like her and her friends? Would she become interested in boys and forget the horse or not have time for her in a year or two? Would La Duquesa stand in her stall day after day waiting for her? Was that in the best interest of the horse?

Sara took another sip of her tea. It was completely cold and now bitter. She had sat staring at a photograph of a lovely horse for the past three hours and still had no idea what to do about it. She begged Aunt Annie to give her some kind of sign. "Please help me, Aunt Annie. I have no idea what the right thing to do is anymore. I wish I could talk it over with you. If you can, please give me some kind of sign, please, please." Tears were streaming again.

Sara got up and took her tea to the kitchen, cleaned the cup and saucer and put them in the cupboard and got out the vacuum cleaner. She decided action was better than inaction and went to work. She re-cleaned the downstairs, shopped for a few groceries to make dinner, and went to bed early. She fell into a restless sleep with the television on.

CHAPTER EIGHTEEN

For several nights after her in-laws showed up in Pinon Hills out of the blue, Rose Wilcox had trouble sleeping at night. She went over and over her conversation with Charles Carnegie about the trust fund he wanted to bestow on her daughter. She was well aware what that kind of money could do for Maryann but she was also aware how destructive it could be. There were examples of that in the news and in the papers every day. Money led to feelings of entitlement in some people. Money led to feelings that one was above the law and could do as they pleased. Maryann was a well-adjusted young lady. She'd not grown up with "money to burn" and she had a good concept of the value of money. She had lived without some of the things money can buy so she appreciated things more when she got them. Would this trust fund upset the foundation Rose and her aunt and uncle had worked so hard to give her? She didn't think so, but would it be worth taking a chance?

Rose woke up on the fourth day with a sore throat and scratchy cough. She ignored it. There had been someone in the hardware store a few days earlier with a child that sneezed everywhere. Maybe she was catching an early spring cold. It happened occasionally. She always got over it in a few days. Rose took some Tylenol with her coffee that morning and went to work as usual. The cough got progressively worse over the next day and a half. Mrs. Andrews came in to the office for some figures for the accountant. She took one look and Rose and asked, "Are you feeling as bad as you look?"

Rose shook her head. "No, I just caught a little cold. I've been taking my vitamin C and Tylenol. I'll be okay in a day or two."

Rose struggled with her "cold" for the next two days. She had periodic coughing fits that began leaving her breathless. Aunt Adele and Roy noticed it and said something to her about taking a day or two off work. She shushed them. "I can't take time off right now. We are in the middle of second quarter close and besides that, I need the money to pay bills." Even Maryann worried about her mom. Adele and Roy took turns driving Maryann to and from school and the ranch so Rose could come directly home after work and rest.

On the third day, Rose was sitting in the back office going over the figures for the accountant when the numbers began swimming on the page. Her body ached all over and felt like it was on fire. Her coughing fits were frequent and left her struggling to breathe. She began coughing up sputum that discolored the Kleenex. She started to think she should go to the doctor. Mrs. Andrews came in for something and found her gripped in another coughing spasm. She noted the Kleenex Rose held to her mouth discolored with a pinkish hue. Rose looked like she was about to pass out when she finally quit coughing. She walked around the desk and put her hand on Rose's forehead.

"You are burning up with fever!" Mrs. Andrews told her. "This isn't a simple cold. We need to get you to the hospital right now." She picked up the phone and dialed 911 ignoring

Rose's protestations. Rose sat back in defeat and waited for the paramedics to arrive.

The paramedics checked Rose's vital signs and agreed with Mrs. Andrews. "We're taking her to the hospital right now," they told her as they put Rose on oxygen and started an IV in her arm. They put Rose on the portable gurney and pushed her in the back of their ambulance. They switched the siren and flashing lights on as they left the parking lot of the hardware store.

Mrs. Andrews called Rose's home telephone number. Roy was the only one there. Adele was picking Maryann up at school and driving her to Hartley Ranch to meet her grandparents. She told Roy what little she knew about Rose's condition and where she was going.

Roy called the ranch and spoke with Ginny. Maryann had not arrived at the ranch yet but her grandparents were there. Ginny hurried outside and let Charles and Celeste know about Rose. They met Maryann at the gate and talked to Adele. Charles suggested he and Celeste take Maryann to the hospital and Adele could pick Roy up on the way and bring him there too. Everyone rushed to the hospital hoping Rose was going to be okay.

When the family arrived at the emergency room, the nurse on duty asked them to wait while the doctor examined Rose. When he had a better idea of Rose's condition, they would let them in to see her two at a time.

Maryann sat in the waiting room with her grandparents and her great uncle and aunt for what seemed to her like hours. At that time, the waiting room was not very busy but the family sat quietly waiting and hoping for good news. Maryann was in shock with fear. Her mother was never sick! She'd had a cold before, but she'd never been taken away in an ambulance. She was scared out of her mind. Tears streamed down her face. Celeste threw her arms around her and held her as she sobbed, comforting her in soothing tones. Adele sat on the other side of Maryann and held her hand. Charles and Roy sat across from them with worried looks on their faces.

The doctor finally popped his head into the waiting room and called, "Family of Rose Wilcox?" Charles and Roy jumped to their feet and rushed to the door. Charles introduced them as Rose's father-in-law and uncle. "Come with me," the doctor told them. He escorted them to a small curtained off room. Rose lay on the bed with an oxygen mask on and her eyes closed. She was so pale she almost disappeared into the bedding. A monitor beeped as it kept track of her breathing, blood pressure, heart rate and blood oxygenation. An IV stand in the corner of the room had tubes snaking down the bed to the IV in her arm, dripping medication.

"She has a serious case of pneumonia. Her left lung is pretty bad, her right lung has some fluid in it as well. We need to keep her here for a few days to get that under control. She's young and in good health otherwise so I don't see a long term problem for her if we get a handle on it now. We've given her medication to help with the coughing and antibiotics for the infection. She's sleepy from the drugs but she is breathing on her own. Her blood oxygenation is a little lower than we like but if it stays where it is we won't have to intubate her. Do you have any questions?"

"Can we bring her daughter in to see her?" Roy asked.

"How old is she?" the doctor queried. "We don't usually let really young ones in here because there's too much contamination in an emergency room. We also don't let kids in here that are sick themselves to avoid making others sick."

"Maryann is 13-years-old and she's not sick at all," Charles answered. "I will be responsible for her," he offered.

Roy and Charles walked back to the waiting room. Roy asked Maryann if she would like to go see her mother. Maryann jumped up and ran to the door. Charles held the door for her, let her enter and took her hand. When he led her to the bed she saw her Mother's face and was frightened more than before. Charles and the doctor patiently explained what was happening in a manner she could understand. Maryann stood close to Charles and he held her with his arm around her shoulders. "Is she going to be okay?" Maryann asked the doctor.

"I think so, young lady. We will keep her here for a few days. We're just waiting for the transfer from here to the ICU upstairs. I'd like to keep her there for a day, maybe a day and a half, to let the medication start doing its work. We'll move her into a regular room as soon as we can. The nurses in ICU won't let you in to see her there but you can come see her when we move her out of the ICU."

Maryann stood for a few minutes holding her mother's hand. Her tears gradually stopped as she watched her mother's chest raise and fall in rhythm with her breathing. She looked at Charles. "Maybe we should go and let Aunt Adele and Grandma see her," she suggested. She bent over and kissed Rose on the cheek. "Mom, we're pulling for you. You just stay here and get better," she whispered. "I love you."

CHAPTER NINETEEN

The next few days were a tangle for everyone but Rose. Charles rented another car so Celeste had her own transportation. Charles and Celeste drove Maryann to school, the ranch, the hospital and home so Roy and Adele didn't use their own money for gas. Their home was a 45-minute drive away from the hospital. Charles or Celeste took them to see Rose. Celeste spent as much time as she could with Rose at the hospital. As soon as she was transferred into a regular room from the ICU, Celeste filled the room with flowers.

When Rose suggested her hospital room was looking like a funeral parlor, Celeste laughed it off. "You need something beautiful to look at, my dear," she said in response.

Rose tried to laugh, ending in a coughing fit. Finally she said, "I guess they are better than the view of the parking lot from this room." Both of them laughed over that.

Charles or Celeste brought home dinner most nights so Adele could go with Celeste and Maryann to visit Rose. They remained in contact with Rose's boss at Andrews Hardware every day with updates on her condition and improvement.

If Adele needed something from the grocery store, Charles brought it home for her. If bills came in for Rose, Charles paid them. If Maryann needed anything for school, Charles or Celeste picked it up for her. They left nothing undone and took care of Roy and Adele as if they were their own aging family members.

Rose hadn't made up her mind about trusting them until she came home from the hospital. She was discharged under doctor's orders to take it easy for at least week and a follow-up visit with her doctor before returning to work. Charles and Celeste did everything. They handled grocery shopping, kid shuttling, bill paying, and anything else that needed doing. They extended their stay in California for as long as it took. Neither of them wanted to leave until they were sure Rose was okay. And they did it all cheerfully without complaint.

On Rose's second night back home, Adele invited Charles and Celeste to a home cooked meal at their home for a change. She was tired of eating other people's cooking and wanted to get her own kitchen up and running again. She made her famous pot roast dinner that night and added two chairs and place settings to the kitchen table. It was a bit cramped but there was room for everyone.

"If I had known you could put out a meal like this," Charles began, "I'd have helped you myself," He laughed. "This is wonderful!"

"Glad you enjoyed it," Adele smiled a bit shyly. "It's a wonder what a few seasonings can do to a cheap cut of meat and a few potatoes and carrots."

"Ah, but the apple pie was a revelation!" Celeste chimed in. "Best I ever had. You and Charles should get together in the kitchen sometime. He's a darned good cook himself you know."

"Really?" Rose said in amazement. "Charles Carnegie cooks?"

"Absolutely!" Celeste smiled at her. "When we first got married, I didn't know how to boil water. We'd have starved if it hadn't been for Charles. His mother had a wonderful cook when he was growing up. He spent a lot of time in the kitchen with her. She taught him a lot more than his mother knew. His mother was one of those who didn't believe in fraternizing with the help. Charles had to sneak into the kitchen to work with her. I thought all that wonderful food coming from my mom's kitchen just appeared out of thin air I guess. I never thought about it until I was married and couldn't tell a frying pan from a tea kettle." She laughed remembering. "When Charles got too busy, I let him hire a cook for us. He knew a lot more about it than I did."

"Oh, by the way, Celeste and I have been talking. We really do need to get back home in a few days to take care of some business there, but we'd like to come back soon if that would be okay with you all," Charles told the group around the dinner table.

"Oh, that would be great, Grandpa. I'm going to miss you when you leave," Maryann said. "Who is going to help Brody and Clyde and me with water buckets when you go home?"

Roy and Adele added their approval with enthusiasm. They truly liked the Carnegies. Rose added her approval to the mix as well.

"We've done some talking. We would like to get a place here for ourselves if it's okay with you Rose," Celeste began. "We would like to come here and spend more time with you and Maryann and, of course, Roy and Adele. We have no family left where we live. And there isn't much that we do there that we can't do from here."

"Oh, that sounds perfect," Maryann interjected. "You can watch me when I show La Duquesa. That will be so fun!"

Everyone was looking at Rose. She sat pensively for a minute. "Charles, you and I need to have a talk, but as far as you and Celeste getting a place close by, I'm all for it. I don't know how Roy and Adele and I could have gotten through the past couple of weeks without you two. I can't thank you enough for all your help."

"Yeah!!" cried Maryann. "I'm gonna have grandparents in the neighborhood! That's great!"

Later that evening, after Maryann was tucked into bed, Rose and Charles had their little chat. Rose agreed to the trust fund transfer and signed the papers needed to get that done. She hugged Charles and thanked him again for all the help during her illness. She had one caveat. She wanted to be the one to tell Maryann about it and she wanted Celeste to help teach her about the responsibilities that come with having money. Twenty seven million dollars is a lot to settle on a thirteen-year-old. She didn't think it would be a good idea to tell her everything at one time.

Charles and Celeste went house hunting the next day. They found a lovely four-bedroom cabin in Wrightwood, just a few minutes from Roy and Adele's house. They paid cash for it and requested a short escrow so they could move in when they returned to California.

Rose made a short appearance at Andrews Hardware to give her notice. Mr. and Mrs. Andrews were sorry to see her go. Rose promised she wouldn't leave them in a lurch. She offered to help hire and train her own replacement. She placed the ad in the local newspaper for them that very day. Once a suitable candidate was found, Rose was ready to return to work and began training her. It didn't take long before Rose was out of a job permanently.

Maryann talked on the phone every evening to Grandpa and Grandma Carnegie. She kept them up to date on the goings on at the ranch, how La Duquesa was doing, what mischief Clyde got into and how the training for the next show was doing. Some of the new tack Ginny special ordered for Maryann showed up and she gushed to her grandparents how nice it was and how much she and Quesa liked it. She also told them about the fittings for her new show clothes and how beautiful they were. She thanked them over and over again for the beautiful things they bought especially for her and La Duquesa. She told them they were the best grandparents in the whole wide world twice or maybe three times over. And she told them she loved them.

CHAPTER TWENTY

The escrow closed on the Wrightwood cabin while Grandma and Grandpa Carnegie were closing up their home on the East Coast and putting things in order so they could return to California. They checked into the same hotel when they got back because Grandma had to furnish their new home. She, Rose and Aunt Adele went on shopping excursions for everything from furniture to bath towels while Maryann was in school. Charles took Roy on a shopping trip for men. They went to the local Jeep dealer and bought five of them. One was for Rose, one for Adele, one for Roy and one for Charles and one for Celeste. Charles wouldn't hear of Roy having to spend another minute under the hood of the "junkers" he and Rose owned and the extra car gave Adele a vehicle of her own. Roy and Charles picked pretty colors for the ladies and nice manly colors for themselves. It was the first taste of luxury Rose, Adele and Roy had experienced for many years. Rose insisted the funds for three of the vehicles come out of the trust fund because all three of them provided transportation for Maryann.

Maryann spent afternoons at Hartley Ranch doing chores with Brody and Clyde. Most days Grandpa joined them, clad in jeans and work boots, well-worn and bearing just the right amount of horse poo to be a rancher according to Brody.

Grandpa enjoyed his time at the ranch. He loved the sweet smell of the grain they measured into buckets for the horses. He loved the smell of alfalfa he helped his granddaughter shove into the Gator for the feed crew. He loved the sparkling clean look of a well-scrubbed water bucket filled with fresh cold water for the horses. He loved the smell of saddle soap and neatsfoot oil and how buttery soft it made leather. When he compared this life to his old one with the sterile environment of a surgical suite and the microscopic surgeries he did to save lives, he had to admit this one won his favor over the other.

Maryann was right about another thing too. Jeans did become softer the more they were washed. They fit his body like another skin, soft and supple. He wore cotton work shirts with pearl buttons on cuffs, pockets and down the front. The shirts absorbed sweat and dirt but fit his body like a glove. The hat became second nature, sweat stained brow band and all. He loved this life! And he loved his granddaughter. It was like he was given a second chance at living and he was taking it on full force.

Grandma also changed a few things. She bought jeans and cotton shirts to wear at the ranch. She bought her first pair of cowgirl boots and a denim jacket for cooler weather. Her jacket had bling all over it to match the new belt she put on with her jeans. The relaxed atmosphere of the ranch settled well on her. She didn't pitch in with the chores but spent her time watching the activities at the ranch especially when Maryann rode. She marveled at how well the horse and rider matched. Celeste had never spent much time outdoors but discovered a whole new world. The high desert sunshine felt good against her skin and she quit worrying about it giving her wrinkles. It just felt too good to be bad for her. The broad vista of the open desert brought a sense of peace to her soul and made her feel at once small and insignificant and a part of the greater scheme of life. She watched jackrabbits and ground squirrels, desert ravens and small mountain jays with the same delight. She felt at peace within herself for the first time in a long time.

Watching their granddaughter practicing on La Duquesa, Charles finally asked Ginny about the possibility of buying the horse for Maryann. Ginny hemmed and hawed for a moment and finally told him the truth. There was a cloud on the ownership of the horse. Yes, she bought and paid for the horse to save it from certain death at the hands of the old drunk. But the horse actually belonged to a young woman who inherited her from the former owner, her aunt. Charles was stumped. He asked what he could do to help. Ginny had no ideas for him then but promised to keep him updated as she got more information. All she had at the moment was the name and phone number of the private investigator the young woman hired to find the horse. She promised Charles she would share that with him if the need arose.

Ginny put the five girls through their paces every Wednesday in a group lesson that began with entering the show ring properly. They had a few days left before the qualifying show that would be their ticket to the Nationals or stop it cold. All five of them were positive they would not miss the opportunity. Ginny watched as one after the other trotted into the arena at a strong trot or jog smiling as if their life depended on it. They each did their best workouts in their discipline. Maryann, the one Ginny pinned her highest hopes on, and La Duquesa entered the arena at a strong English trot looking like the horse was dancing on air. It was beautiful to watch. Maryann and La Duquesa put on their best performance every time. No wrong leads at the canter, no counter canters, no cross posting, perfect changes of gait and perfect halts that didn't leave a puff of dust in their wake. Maryann seemed to know intuitively whether to slow down or speed up just a bit to keep herself in the open in front of the judge and not allow another rider to hide her on the rail. She could cut corners when needed to keep herself and her horse out in the open without being obvious. She didn't need to pull herself off the rail to remain in the open. But there were only five girls in the "class" here at the ranch. It would be entirely different in the real show ring with more competitors.

The fittings for Maryann's day-coats and jodhpurs went well and they arrived finished and ready for her days before the show. She tried them on in Ginny's bedroom so she could show Grandpa and Grandma. Ginny went ahead and ordered three separate day-coats and three pairs of jods for Maryann. Along with the three blouses, that gave her three complete outfits to wear in case one of anything got dirty. She had a lovely raspberry colored day-coat with long tails, a long teal striped one and a beautiful long black one that would look fabulous on the silver coat of La Duquesa. Ginny ordered the jods in black and deep navy blue because they were interchangeable with the coats. The blouses were all white with self-ties. Ginny found pins for each of them. She bought one derby in deep navy blue and one in black so they matched the jods. She bought Maryann the cute hairnet pieces that would keep her long ponytail off the back of her jacket and out of the way, looking neat and tidy. Maryann and her horse were ready for competition.

Move-in day for the show came the day before the first classes of a three day show. The horse trailers, trucks and cars were packed late on Wednesday so the competitors could get a good night's sleep. Thursday morning everyone came to the ranch early for the 90-mile drive to the show grounds. The girls were giddy with excitement. They arrived at the show grounds and bedded the stalls before unloading the horses and putting them away. Then the fun began. All the equipment and tack was unloaded and put away in the tack and ready-rooms in an organized fashion. Ginny directed traffic in that area. Stall drapes were hung. The girls decided beforehand they would stay with their horses on the grounds so their overnight kits, sleeping bags and folding cots were tucked away. It took several hours to get everything organized. Once that was done, each girl took her horse out for a quick practice in the large arena with Ginny to coach them one more time. Mothers, fathers, grandparents and siblings watched. Heidi picked up the wrong lead at the lope and slapped her forehead, stopped her horse and began again. Susie missed her diagonal and had to stop and start over. They were all nervous and excited. Friday morning was the Showmanship classes. Ginny took the girls and their horses near the barn and schooled them over and over again in the pattern they needed to complete without flaw.

Friday morning arrived with a flurry of activity. The girls crawled out of their sleeping bags by five in the morning. They went to the public showers and cleaned up, brushed their teeth and combed their hair laughing and kidding each other. They took their horses out of their stalls and headed for the wash racks carrying shampoo and conditioner and hoses for bathing. They pulled coolers over their damp horses and put them back in their stalls and fed them breakfast. Moms, Dads, grandparents, siblings and Ginny arrived from the local hotel and brought breakfast for the girls to eat while their horses dried. Silly laughing and joking continued because the competitors were in high spirits. Each girl got serious when it came to grooming their horse for show. Horses were brushed within an inch of their lives.

Hooves were sanded with fine grit sandpaper, wiped down and polished with hoof polish so they shined like patent leather. Manes and tails were combed and detangled. Faces needed to be touched up and groomed, saddles and bridles put on. The horses were held by someone else while the girls got into their show clothes for the class. The girls checked each other to be sure the numbers pinned to their jacket backs were correct. Ginny took a few minutes to talk to them as a group and remind them of the pattern they needed to perform without a mistake. Class was called over the loud-speaker. Each of the girls from Ginny's ranch walked toward the arena with their hearts in their throats hoping they would remember the pattern and perform it correctly.

The girls were judged one at a time along with the other exhibitors in the class. It took a while for the judge to get through them all. The ones already judged stood at attention until the last horse and handler were judged and the judge handed in her card to the ring steward. The ring steward called the results to the announcer. He congratulated the class and began by awarding the eighth place. It was not one of Ginny's group. He reached sixth place before one of Ginny's competitors received a ribbon. Susie had mixed up one part of the pattern and knew it when she did it so it didn't surprise her to get sixth place. Fourth, Third, Second and First places were awarded to Ginny's girls with Maryann getting the First. Except for Fifth place, they'd swept the competition with Maryann leading the group! Everyone congratulated Ginny and the girls for one of the best Showmanship classes they'd seen. The girls were wild with excitement and ready for the rest of the show.

Maryann had the best show of her short life that weekend. Every class she entered with La Duquesa they won hands down. She and Quesa were the very best they could be. Ginny stood on the sideline and watched every move they made. She had one or two suggestions that would improve their performance at Nationals but they were minor things. Spectators around the ring watched in awe and came to see the pair when their classes were over. The combination of Maryann and La Duquesa was perfect. La Duquesa was flawless. When she trotted on, it looked like she was dancing. While Maryann rode her she became part of her, more than her partner, and it was beautiful to watch. Becky arrived with her mother before Maryann's first class so she was on the sidelines hanging onto the rail cheering her on. When her classes were over, Becky was hanging onto La Duquesa and telling Maryann how wonderful they looked together. That meant a lot to Maryann.

Ginny was very pleased. Maryann, Melissa, Susie, Heidi and Kathy all qualified to show at the Youth National Championships with a first or second place in their divisions. The cloud on La Duquesa's ownership was the only thing that worried her.

CHAPTER TWENTY-ONE

G inny worried more and more about her claim on La Duquesa. She'd seen the will. Anne Stone had been one of her favorite professors when she was in college. She had a lot of respect for her. She couldn't figure out how La Duquesa was left in the situation she and Mike found her in. Watching Maryann and La Duquesa at the show over the weekend strengthened her feeling that the two of them belonged together. There was no doubt in her mind. And Maryann now had the support of her grandparents, so it wasn't that she couldn't afford to keep her own horse.

Grandpa and Grandma Carnegie talked about the situation as well. Charles was used to getting whatever he wanted because he'd always had enough money to buy it. Watching Maryann and La Duquesa at the horse show over the weekend solidified his resolve to make sure the horse became Maryann's. He didn't want to push Ginny Hartley too hard.

Sara Evans stayed housebound in the home that belonged to her Aunt Annie for several days after her phone conversation with Charlie Spade. She couldn't make up her mind what was the best course of action. Her Aunt specifically left La Duquesa in her care and she'd blown it right off the bat. The guilt made her feel ill. The more she thought about the situation, the more she wanted to see La Duquesa herself to be sure she was healthy and happy where she was. Sara called Charlie Spade and asked him if he would take her to Hartley Ranch. He promised her a call back when he had an appointment with Mrs. Hartley.

Charlie Spade called Ginny right away. "My client would like to come up and see La Duquesa as soon as possible," he began. "I think she is having second thoughts about the horse. I not sure what her thinking is at the moment, but can I suggest I bring her up to your ranch at a time when she can see that young lady working with her. That might be the tipping point for her."

When Charlie called Sara to confirm the time, she called Tania and asked her to join them. She wanted the opinion of a professional. Aunt Annie trusted Tania so she would be the perfect one to give her opinion to Sara.

Charlie, Sara and Tania arrived at the ranch after school let out and Ginny's five girls were in the barn getting their horses ready for another Wednesday afternoon session. Ginny was surprised to see Tania. "Well, I haven't seen you for a while," she said greeting her. "How long has it been anyway?"

Ginny and Tania compared notes for a few minutes. "You know that I'm the one who saddle- trained La Duquesa, don't you?" Tania asked. "We qualified her in two shows and took her to the National Championships last year, just before Anne was diagnosed with terminal cancer."

"I had no idea," Ginny told her. "I knew when I first began working with her that someone with skill had worked with her before. That explains a lot to me. You're one of the best trainers in the area."

Tania told Ginny about the first owners and how Anne Stone fell in love with La Duquesa the first time she saw her. "She pulled me aside and asked me to let her know if Quesa ever became available. It surprised me. She was one of my professors at school too. I knew she'd never owned a horse of her own before. Guess it was just the combination of beauty and chemistry!"

"How long did Anne own Quesa?" Ginny asked.

"The first owners had a financial set back right after the regional show. The husband lost his job and they couldn't afford to keep her and show her so they asked me to make inquiries. I only made one phone call that night and the deal was done within a couple of days. I'd never seen Anne Stone so smitten with a horse before," Tania laughed. "She was like a teen-aged girl, all giggly. It was actually funny."

"What I don't understand is how she got in the condition Mike and I found her," Ginny said somberly. "I'm convinced she would have died within a few days if we hadn't come along. Our dog, Clyde, was with us on one of our infrequent trail rides and heard something we didn't hear. He took off and went after the man who was beating her. That's when I decided to buy her to get her out of there. If we couldn't save her, at least that person wouldn't be the last thing she ever saw and she would know someone cared about her."

"I have to accept the blame for that," Sara interjected sadly. "The day my aunt passed away, I had quite a bit to get through despite my own grief. I called Tania to come and pick her up at the cabin, finished what I needed to do there and left. I forgot to follow up with Tania. I didn't know Aunt Annie's absentee husband was going to move right on into the cabin like that. I never checked on the cabin. I dropped the ball and it almost cost La Duquesa her life."

Charlie said to her, "Miss Evans, anyone could miss something when we are overwhelmed by a death in the family like you experienced. Don't beat yourself up over it. It worked out in the end."

"Listen folks, I have a lesson to give. Why don't you three have a seat on the deck and watch us. These five young ladies all qualified to show at the Youth Nationals and they are rearing to go. Maryann's grandparents should be here any minute," Ginny told them. She strode off toward the arena and walked into the center. Brody came over and opened the gate for the girls who were sitting mounted and ready.

The lesson began with each girl making their perfect entrance into the show ring. When it was Maryann's and La Duquesa's turn, Maryann cued her to a strong trot and smiled big enough for the group on the patio to see. She looked like she was having the time of her life, which she actually was at the moment.

Tania's mouth dropped open. "Wow! I've never seen Quesa move like that! I saddle- trained her and showed her myself, but that's unbelievable. Look what that young lady gets out of that horse, will ya? That's one happy horse if I've ever seen one!"

Sara and Charlie Spade were not horse people but they couldn't help but see what a perfect duo Maryann and La Duquesa made right in front of their eyes. They were beautiful together despite the torn jeans and tee-shirt Maryann wore with her ponytail flipping up and down in time to the horse's strides. They watched the girls put their horses through their paces for a while.

"I think I've seen enough here," Sara finally admitted. "La Duquesa looks wonderful and she's obviously been well cared for here. Let's go."

Charlie Spade waved goodbye to Ginny as soon as he caught her eye. The group turned and left before Charles and Celeste Carnegie arrived.

Ginny was puzzled. Why didn't they wait? Why rush off like that? What was Sara Evans thinking now? She had no idea. She talked to Charles about the visit after the lesson. "Mr. Spade told me Sara Evans wanted to see La Duquesa so we made an appointment for a time when she could see the mare working with Maryann. They weren't here very long. I don't know if she's made a decision on the situation."

Charles had a worried look on his face. "They couldn't have been here very long. I was hoping to meet them myself. Then again, maybe she saw what we've all seen. It certainly is obvious to everyone else."

La Duquesa saw Sara Evans. She wondered what she was doing there. She didn't stay long. She didn't stop to see her in the barn either. Would this mean she would be moving away soon and losing contact with Maryann? She hoped not with all her heart but she'd lost people before. She loved Ginny and Brody and Clyde too. She didn't want to move away from any of them.

The next chance she had, she talked to Clyde about it to see if he knew anything. "*I heard they were coming over and wanted to see you and Maryann,*" Clyde told her. "*You are looking lovely now. Maybe that's what she wanted to see. Ginny hasn't said much but I heard her talking with Mike about it and she seemed nervous.*"

"*Oh, that makes me feel better,*" Quesa said almost sarcastically.

"*Now don't get your tail in a tangle. You know people say one thing when they mean just the opposite all the time,*" Clyde quipped. "*Besides, I'm pretty sure Maryann's grandparents wouldn't let you go. They know how much Maryann loves you.*"

"*Well, maybe I'd better pay special attention to them then. Her grandmother doesn't come to the barn much. I don't think she likes to get dirty or smell like a horse. But her grandfather* comes in here all the time. I will make an effort to be sweet to him," Quesa suggested.

"Wouldn't hurt," Clyde agreed with her before dashing out of the barn to chase a pesky squirrel away from the feed room.

CHAPTER TWENTY-TWO

On the drive from Pinon Hills to Redlands, Sara Evans was quiet, reflecting on what she'd seen at Hartley Ranch. La Duquesa didn't look worse for the wear, she looked better than ever if that was possible. She looked happy. So did Maryann. Maybe Sara should take Charlie Spade's advice and just let her go. But other thoughts crowded in. What happens in a couple of years when Maryann finds a boyfriend? Will she leave La Duquesa standing in her stall day after day because she doesn't have time for her anymore? What about what her aunt wanted? She'd left the horse for Sara in her will. Did that mean Sara should get more involved in her life? Did that mean her aunt wanted her to become an equestrian in the long run? Did that give her permission to gift the horse to another person more suited to her? She shook her head. She needed to make a decision and it needed to be done soon. If she took the mare, she didn't want to break Maryann's heart but maybe she should do it before Maryann got even more attached to La Duquesa. She didn't have an answer. She silently asked Aunt Annie to give her a sign. "Please tell me what is the right thing to do?" Then she felt guilty again for not being able to make a darned decision on her own. She went home and made herself a cup of tea and sat in Aunt Annie's living room staring at the photograph of La Duquesa. She was immobilized by her own inability to decide.

She sat there for a long time just staring at the photograph. Suddenly the shadow-box frame that held La Duquesa's roses and ribbons from her National Championship ride fell off the wall striking the mantle. The glass smashed into a million pieces all over the living room. Sara jumped out of her skin in shock and surprise. "Holy Cow! Aunt Annie is this your way of giving me a sign?" she asked. "What is that supposed to mean?"

Sara picked up the broken frame and tucked the ribbons and roses inside it and took it out to the garage. She would take it back to the frame shop and have it repaired when she had time. She hauled out the vacuum cleaner and cleaned up the mess. She spent the balance of the day in a quandary. What was Aunt Annie trying to tell her?

Charles Carnegie got the phone number for Charlie Spade from Ginny and gave him a call the next day. He introduced himself and expressed his disappointment that he hadn't actually met him at the ranch. "We were surprised to find you'd already been there and gone before we got there. I was hoping to talk with Miss Evans myself," Charles explained.

Charlie Spade told him Sara wanted to see the horse for herself. "I think she's trying to make up her mind what to do about the situation. She knows what happened to La Duquesa and she wanted to see for herself that the horse is well and happy. She doesn't seem like a person who enjoys horses much so I'm guessing she will probably give up her claim now that she's seen for herself."

"Well, you could see how much my granddaughter loves that horse. If it comes down to money, I can solve that problem quickly and easily. All you have to do is give me a number," Charles told him.

Charles talked to Celeste and Ginny after the phone call. "Maybe she really doesn't want the horse for herself. Her investigator believes she is probably going to give up her claim on La Duquesa. I told him I would take care of it if it becomes a question of the money," he told them. "Let's hope he's right and she just wanted to check on the horse's welfare."

Sara walked around for the next week deciding to give up her claim for the horse one minute and deciding to start taking riding lessons on her the next. She could always put La Duquesa back with Tania. She would be well cared for there. But what if she met a nice man and didn't have time for the horse herself? And so she vacillated.

Maryann and Becky began talking about the Youth Nationals competition in earnest. Maryann was completely in the dark about the ownership issues with La Duquesa. Ginny bought the mare and owned her but was letting Maryann show her. That was all she knew and the adults around her were careful not to let on.

Grandpa and Grandma Carnegie went to San Juan Capistrano several times when Maryann went with Ginny to ride Prince Ali for Becky. He was fit and ready to go. Becky's doctor finally gave her permission to ride again so long as she wore a helmet to protect her head. Ginny began hauling La Duquesa to San Juan so Becky and Maryann could practice together in the arena.

The girls had time to talk about all the events that would go on during Youth Nationals from the barn decorating contest to ice cream socials and judging competitions. Maryann came up with an idea for barn decorating. She suggested she paint portraits of the horses attending from Chris O'Neal's barn and Ginny's barn and make them look like movie posters. They could use "movies" as the theme.

Becky loved the idea. They got Todd O'Neal on the phone in Colorado to talk about it. He agreed with them. He sent photos to Maryann on her phone so she could see the horses they were bringing.

Maryann didn't have much time to paint all the portraits so she talked to her Mom that night about the supplies she needed. She asked her if they could afford the poster boards, paints, brushes and maybe poster frames. She had no idea what their financial situation was but knew her mom was no longer working. She assumed her grandparents paid for the new cars in the driveway. Maryann knew her grandparents were helping them but had no idea she was sitting on twenty-seven million dollars. She wasn't sure they could afford what she needed. She wanted to have time to ask the others competing if she needed their help with the money. She'd already talked to everyone and they all thought "movies" was a great idea for barn decorations. Some of the high desert girls were painting gold star shapes to stick on the barns. Todd and his friends were getting together to construct a few other touches. Chris O'Neal and Ginny talked to the local plant man in Albuquerque for specific plants they could rent to go with the theme.

Rose hadn't talked to Maryann about her trust fund yet. She spent mornings with Charles and Celeste going over details. They set up a bank account locally for a part of the funds. She'd just gotten the blank checks from the bank on that account that morning. Rose surprised Maryann by asking for a list of things she needed and promised to get them all for her the next day while she was in school.

Maryann was excited that she could start the paintings after dinner tomorrow night. School was almost over for the year and the teachers were not giving much homework. There were final exams coming up, but Maryann wasn't worried about them. She'd aced her classes all year so she knew the material.

Maryann started painting the first poster of Prince Ali and Becky. She showed the horse dressed in his Native Costume and titled the "movie" Prince Ali – Sheik of the Desert. Maryann's depiction of Prince Ali was very good and the poster looked nearly professional in quality. She was pleased with it. Her next poster was for Todd O'Neal and his bay gelding Desperado. Naturally she used a Wild West theme for that one because Desperado was a western horse. There had to be long horn cattle in the background. Heidi's hunter gelding was painted with the fox hounds. She painted La Duquesa with herself riding in a long ruffled gown and wearing a hair comb under a long lace head covering.

Sara Evans still had not decided what to do a week after seeing La Duquesa at Hartley Ranch. She called Tania for her opinion. She got it.

"Honestly, Sara, you're not a horse person. You don't have the passion for one. You don't know how to ride and never tried. I know Anne gave you the horse. She made you the custodian but you need to do the right thing for her now. You've seen how that mare works for Maryann. You've seen how much Maryann loves her and really has a passion for her. What else do you need to know? Get off the dime and do the right thing! For the love of Heaven, if Anne Stone could see what we did a week ago, she would agree. Maryann should have that horse!" Tania told her. "Maryann put time and energy into a filthy, starving, scared out of her mind horse. She turned her into what we saw. It's high time you made that little girl's dreams come true and stop putting roadblocks up against them."

Charles was chafing at the bit about the Sara Evans situation too. He waited a week and called Charlie Spade again. "Would you please offer Miss Evans twenty-five thousand dollars and see if that will change her mind," he asked him. Charlie agreed to call his client with the offer. He dialed the phone just as she was about to make a call herself.

"Sara, you have an offer for La Duquesa. Charles Carnegie just got off the phone with me. He is Maryann Wilcox's grandfather. He offered you twenty-five thousand dollars for her. That would be a legitimate sale and relieve you of the responsibility for the horse," Charlie told her.

Sara was relieved. It would be doing the right thing for La Duquesa and it was a good price for her too. After the tongue lashing she'd gotten from Tania last night, she had to admit this felt good to her. "Done," was her answer to Charlie.

When Charles got off the phone with Charlie the second time, he talked with Ginny and got copies of the will from her. He faxed them to his attorney with instructions to draw up the papers and get them over-night to Sara Evans along with a certified check. That cleared up the cloud on the ownership of La Duquesa. Virginia Hartley would be the owner free and clear. However, that still didn't get La Duquesa to Maryann as her personal horse.

Charles had another conversation with Ginny that morning. "I'm going to make you the same offer I made Sara Evans. I will pay you twenty-five thousand dollars for La Duquesa so Celeste and I can give her to our granddaughter. Will you accept?"

Ginny looked at him like he'd just grown a third eye in the middle of his forehead. "What are you talking about?" she asked.

"I've just cleared up the ownership issue with La Duquesa. Now I want to buy her for my granddaughter and I'm making you an offer," he told her seriously.

"Charles, that would cost you fifty-thousand dollars for one horse. Are you kidding me?" Ginny asked him.

Charles laughed. "Look, I paid one hundred and sixteen thousand dollars for a polo pony for my son twenty or twenty-five years ago. This sounds like a better deal to me and I think I just bought a better horse in the bargain," Charles smiled at her.

"Well, that sure makes the five hundred dollars I invested turn a good profit doesn't it?" she smiled back at him.

"Ginny, the important part is I want to give that horse to Maryann, but on my terms. I don't want her to know anything about this until we are ready to hand her the papers. Can you work with me on this?" Charles asked.

"Anything you want," she replied and hugged him.

CHAPTER TWENTY-THREE

L a Duquesa had plenty of time to think about her life. She fondly remembered the grassy pasture she and her mother were turned out in when she was a tiny baby. She remembered playing with other foals, running and stretching her legs, squealing with delight in the early spring sunshine. She remembered the grooms that handled her and her mother. They were kind and gentle with her while teaching her about halters and how to lead behind her mother. She daydreamed about that sometimes. It was a happy time for her.

Then she remembered the new owners. They'd stuffed her in a dark trailer and shut the door, separating her from her mother who was screaming for her as they drove off. The drive to her new home was frightening. The box she was shut up in moved and jerked, making it difficult for her to maintain her balance. When the trailer finally stopped, the two of them manhandled her into a fenced lot with a small shelter and no other horse in sight. They left her there for almost three years. Her only companions had been one old dog and two sweet goats in the fenced lot next to hers.

The dog would lie down beside her sometimes when she was the most lonely and depressed. He didn't have much to say but was kind to her. The only time the couple spent with her was to brush her before the farrier came to trim her feet or the veterinarian came once each year to give her a check-up and vaccinations. The farrier was kind and patient with her teaching her how to stand on three legs while he worked on one hoof at a time. The vet was also nice to her, gentle and seemed to care about her but he was only there one time each year.

Then she met Tania. Tania picked her up and took her to a new place where there were other horses. Tania spent time with her teaching her new things. She taught her about bathing and how good it felt to be clean and brushed. She exercised her until her body felt strong and powerful. She taught her about bridles and bits in a way that didn't scare her. She taught her about having someone sit on her back and guide her with legs and reins. And sometimes she just spent time with her and talked to her. That was the second best time she'd had. She felt cared for and respected, and maybe loved a little bit. But Tania also had other horses to care for. La Duquesa came to treasure the time Tania spent alone with her.

Tania put her in the trailer and took her to her first horse show. There were many horses there, some of which were nervous like she was. It was a new place. It smelled of other horses. Tania tacked her up and rode her in a large arena for practice. Other horses were there too riding in different disciplines. She didn't want to let Tania down for anything in the world. She concentrated hard to do exactly what Tania asked of her. When her class came, Tania spent extra time grooming her and getting her ready. Tania's tension was evident to Quesa despite Tania's assurances. She knew something important was about to happen. When Tania cued her to trot through the gate that time, other horses were already in the arena and others came in behind her. She knew something was different. She concentrated even harder so she wouldn't let Tania down. She did exactly what Tania asked her to do and forgot the noise and horses all around her. She set her head and neck as Tania taught her and stared straight ahead, moving as she was asked. Then she stood quietly in the center of the arena while the judge walked past the line of horses and scribbled notes on a pad in her hand. The announcer called numbers and names of horses and riders and they left the lineup heading for the out-gate. La Duquesa heard her own name called at last. Tania squealed and threw her arms around La Duquesa before asking her to walk to the out-gate. She stopped her short while a lady came and pinned a blue ribbon to her bridle. Tania cued her into her strong trot once more and they made a pass around the arena while people outside cheered. La Duquesa didn't know what all the fuss was about but did as she was asked. Her owners were waiting at the gate for her and pulled the ribbon off her bridle. They were absolutely silly over a piece of blue ribbon. She didn't understand at all. Back at her stall, Miss Annie came to see her.

There was something different about Miss Annie right from the start. Quesa felt it immediately. Miss Annie came to see her often and brought horse cookies, apples or carrots. She talked to her and brushed her. Sometimes she turned her out in the arena to stretch her legs and Miss Annie stood against the rail to watch. Her eyes were soft and conveyed a message Quesa never felt before. It was love. Oh, she knew her mother loved her but that was so long ago she'd almost forgotten what that felt like.

One day Miss Annie came to see her and threw her arms around her neck squealing with happiness. "You're mine now! All mine!" The joy in her face was infectious. La

Duquesa felt a joy sweep through her own body. She had her own "heart-human" now. She belonged to Miss Annie.

Annie took her to where she worked and Tania came to work with her there. There were many horses at that place and many young people too. Annie spoiled her with attention. The young people she called her students did as well. She felt a different kind of love. La Duquesa was truly happy.

Annie and Tania took her to two more horse shows, one not far away and one very far away. Annie was not as concerned about the ribbons La Duquesa won as her first owners were but was so happy about her performances she was bursting with pride when other people came to see her. She spent special time with La Duquesa, just the two of them.

La Duquesa was the first one to notice when Annie got sick. Even Annie tried to ignore it. They ended up at the cabin. Quesa's stall was right outside Annie's bedroom window so she could see her. When the weather was good the window was opened and she could hear her. Annie talked to her when she was strong enough. Quesa saw the parade of nurses come and go. Sara Evans stayed to help Annie. She came out to feed and brush Quesa. She put her winter coat on every night and took it off in the morning if the weather was warmer. She was kind to Quesa but there was no special feeling from her.

La Duquesa was looking in the window at Miss Annie when she died. Quesa knew when it happened. A light went out inside of her too. She was distraught. She'd never had something or someone die on her. But she knew Annie would never call her name again in the loving tone she used every day.

La Duquesa saw the men carry Annie's body from the cabin covered in a white sheet. She saw Sara leave and drive away. She saw Reilly Stone drive up to the cabin a few hours later. And her life changed completely. She struggled through days and nights of torment from the evil man, often trying to decide if she should just lie down in the mud and quit breathing to make it all stop. Then one day Clyde came charging over the ridge and attacked the man, trying desperately to bite him. And Miss Ginny came into her life.

The look on Miss Ginny's face when she first saw La Duquesa standing in the mud shaking told her more than words would ever tell. Miss Ginny counted some scraps of paper into the man's hand and took a piece of paper from him. He disappeared inside the cabin and Quesa never saw him again.

Miss Ginny walked her out of the quagmire and up to the horse trailer. There was food inside. La Duquesa hadn't seen food for days. She walked right in and became part of Miss Ginny's life.

Miss Ginny was gentle and kind to her always. She felt cared for again. She began to have hope. Then little Maryann crept into her stall and slid down the wall, crunched herself up under the corner feeder and took out her book. She began reading it to Quesa. That was the moment Quesa knew. She knew this little person would be the most important person in her life. She knew Maryann loved her even more than Miss Annie. There was a connection between them that defied gravity, time and space.

CHAPTER TWENTY-FOUR

L a Duquesa was concerned about Sara Evans showing up at the ranch but she was also concerned about Tania being there with her. What did that mean for her? She took every opportunity she could to talk with Clyde about it. He had access to the house and could overhear people talking. They usually ignored the dog unless they were petting him or he was getting in their way or doing something he shouldn't. She sometimes wished she could be as invisible as he was and could go wherever she wanted like he did.

"*Any news about the visitors?*" she asked him the next time he was in the barn.

"*I just get bits and pieces. I know Ginny was nervous about her coming here but not sure what that was about. She didn't say much, even to Mike. But I know she's had a couple of conversations with Grandpa and Grandma. I think they're up to something,*" he told her while he sat and scratched behind his ear.

"*Do you have any idea what?*" La Duquesa asked more concerned than ever.

"*Nope, but I think it has something to do with Maryann so you shouldn't worry your pretty head about it,*" he said.

"You know Grandpa and Grandma love her so it wouldn't be something bad I'm sure."

"Okay. I guess we'll just have to wait and see," was all she could think of.

"With that big horse show coming up, everybody is planning something, you know. It's a big deal for these people. Have you ever been to the National Championships?" he asked her.

"Actually I have. I went last year with Miss Annie and Tania," she answered.

"Who's Miss Annie?" Clyde tilted his head as he asked. He'd not heard that name before.

"She was my owner that died," Quesa answered sadly.

"Oh, gosh. I didn't know. I'm so sorry. It sometimes works out badly for us animals when our person dies, doesn't it?"

"Well, you were my savior when awful things happened to me after she died. I can't thank you enough for that. I'm here. I didn't die myself although I often wished I could. And I found Maryann. I'm so lucky!" she told him. *"You're one of the best friends a lady can have."*

Clyde chuffed. *"Well, if I hear anything I will let you know. But in the meantime just keep on doing what you do. Even I enjoy watching you and Maryann riding together. You look like you are having so much fun, I envy you sometimes,"* he told her, *"but I'm not sure I'd like that thing in my mouth. Seems like it would hurt your teeth."*

"We horses don't have teeth where the bit fits. We just have teeth in the front and teeth in the back. That's because we are grass eaters, not meat eaters like you. Didn't you know that?" she explained. She opened her mouth to show him and pulled her tongue to one side.

"Oh, well, don't you know! I've learned something new today. Thanks!" Clyde grinned at her. Then he caught sight of that pesky squirrel that kept trying to get in the feed room and charged out of the barn like a cat with its tail on fire in hot

pursuit. Quesa thought that was the problem with dogs. They were easily distracted. It was hard to have a conversation with them sometimes.

Suddenly La Duquesa heard a car door shut and heard Maryann's voice calling out for Brody. She got excited all over again. She would be seeing her in a few minutes. Brody called out for Clyde as the two headed for the barn. Maryann walked in and opened the little plastic baggie she had and handed Quesa her treats right away. She always brought chunks of apple or carrot or horse cookies when she came to the ranch. Quesa enjoyed the treats, but enjoyed Maryann's company even more. Maryann got her halter and lead rope on her and led her to the arena for some exercise. She turned La Duquesa out and shut the gate, hurrying back to the barn to get her chores done so she could ride when they finished.

While Maryann and Brody scrubbed water buckets, Clyde splashed in the water and rolled in the dirt. The two laughed at the dog that turned from black to gray with the covering of mud. He stopped hopping around and shook himself from stem to stern tossing mud around in an eight foot circle, splattering it on Maryann and Brody in the process.

"Oh, gross!" Maryann said as she tried to wipe mud off her pants. Clyde sat down and grinned up at her like she said something funny.

"Hey, Brody, why aren't you riding a horse at the National Championships with us?" she asked him out of curiosity.

"I don't have a horse of my own," he answered.

"I don't either, but Aunt Ginny is letting me ride La Duquesa for her. Isn't there one around here that you could ride?" she asked.

"Not really," he said. "Bobbie is the only one that has the training and he's getting old. Besides, Aunt Ginny uses him to teach all the new riders here."

"Haven't you ever had your own horse?" she asked incredulously. She looked around at the ranch full of horses, barns, cows, arenas and outbuildings. There would be plenty of space for Brody to keep one horse for himself, wouldn't there be? She didn't understand.

"My Aunt and Uncle have been really good to me. They have all these horses around and it just seemed like it would be an imposition on them for me to keep one just for myself," he told her.

"Haven't you ever wanted one just for you?" she asked.

"Yeah, I guess. There was one before you came here that I liked a lot. She was a pretty little half-Arabian. Her mother was a beautiful chestnut Arabian that was brought in here to be bred to one of my uncle's Buckskin Paint horses. The filly was born here and stayed here until the owner had her trained and took her home. I just loved that little filly. She used to suck on my fingers before she was weaned. She was pretty as a picture. Her face looked like her mother with great big brown eyes. Uncle Mike had her cutting cows before she was five years old and she was really good at it. I called her my Bizzy Izzy. I really loved her, but she belonged to one of Uncle Mike's clients. You might remember them. They are the Garcia's and they're from Spain. I never got a chance to ride her. She was just gone one day when I got home from school. I don't think Aunt Ginny or Uncle Mike knew how I felt about her and they never said anything to me about her leaving. She was just gone and I've never seen her since." He looked sad when he finished telling the story. "I try not to pay too much attention to the training horses now. I don't want to get attached and then have them leave here so I never get to see them again, ya know."

Maryann was surprised by his answer. She didn't know what to say. She felt sorry for Brody and hoped he would find his "heart horse" someday. Maybe there was something she could do to help. She would talk to Grandpa about it.

CHAPTER TWENTY-FIVE

School was finally over for the year! Maryann passed her finals with flying colors. So did the other girls who rode with her. Their parents all had a special clause they could use if grades dropped. Bad Grades = No Riding! But with summer vacation on for the year, the girls had just about a month before the Youth National Championships to get ready. Every one of the girls at Ginny's ranch wanted to win. They were all "In it to Win it!" That changed schedules a lot. Rose helped pick up some of the other girls whose parents worked during the day so they could work out at the ranch in the early morning hours before it got too hot. Three or four times a week they also got together in the evenings to ride under the arena lights when it was too hot during the middle of the day. Summer afternoon temperatures were often in the high 90's or low 100's and it was too hot to ride and concentrate. The girls spent their afternoons at one another's homes working on their barn decorating projects.

The glittery gold stars were finished up and hooks put on the backs so they could randomly hang them over the stall drapes on the barn walls. Maryann was almost finished with the "movie" posters of the kids with their horses and everyone loved them. Stall signs were under construction now. Wood was cut down to size, then painted in a background color. Maryann drew lettering on them in pencil so the other girls could finish them with painted letters. They made signs for each horse, the tack rooms and the ready rooms where the final grooming and tacking up took place. Todd O'Neal was working with his dad and another boy on some projects in Colorado that would go along with the "movies" theme for their barn decorations. The kids sent pictures back and forth to each other on their cellphones.

Grandma Carnegie arranged a special deal for everyone at a hotel where she knew the owner. It was also the fanciest hotel in town. For Motel 6 prices, they got luxury suites with a hot tub, pool, spa, room service and three fine restaurants on the property. The parents were thrilled. It would be the nicest place any of them stayed at a horse show and it saved them money. The Moms talked about getting together for some spa time while they were there. No sense in wasting a perk like that.

As the days ticked off on the calendars, Maryann became a bit more anxious. She wanted to do well at this competition for a number of reasons. She wanted to make Aunt Ginny proud that she loaned La Duquesa to her to ride. She wanted to make her mother, Aunt and Uncle and Grandparents proud too. But she most especially wanted La Duquesa to be happy. She heard from Aunt Ginny that La Duquesa had already won at the Nationals last year with Tania. This would be her first time at the National Championships. She hoped she could be just as good as Tania.

The Youth National Championship show was held at the New Mexico State Fair complex. There were several arenas that would be used simultaneously throughout the week long competition. With Ginny's five girls, she would be shuttling from arena to arena as their coach for the entire week. She shared a map of the show grounds with Charles and Celeste and pointed out the different arenas where the kids would be performing. Charles looked it over and made a phone call. He rented two six-passenger golf carts for the duration of the show and told Ginny about it. "Walking all that way would probably kill Celeste and I for one and you for the other so I provided transportation they will allow on the grounds for us," he told her laughing.

It hadn't occurred to Ginny but she thanked him profusely. "You probably saved my life!" she told him as she rushed over and hugged him, planting a kiss on his cheek.

The week before the trip everyone began their lists of things they needed so they wouldn't forget anything important. Each girl had her own and Ginny had a master one for the tack, feed and ready rooms. All supplies they needed to take were procured and stored in a single place in Ginny's tack room until packing day. All the decorations were stored there as well.

Packing day came. Everyone got to the ranch early and began packing trucks, cars, and trailers with everything but the horses. They worked through the morning to be sure nothing was missed. They finished up later in the afternoon when the last bundle was stowed. The stalls in the trailers were bedded. Water for the trip was in full storage containers in each trailer along with feed for the trip itself. Feed for the week was in truck beds and on a flatbed trailer one of the trucks would haul.

The amount of gear stored was incredible. They had to take enough hay, grain and supplements for five horses for a 14-day period. They added all the bottles of shampoo, conditioner, hoses, and coolers for bathing five horses daily. Then they added all the show tack for horses riding different disciplines and the work tack for warming them up and keeping them fit and healthy. Next came all the show clothes the girls needed to wear while showing them with spares in case something got dirty or torn. On top of that was the luggage containing clothes and toiletries for each person traveling with the group. They couldn't forget all the barn decorations they needed for the "movies" theme for the show barns. When they finished packing, the line of trucks and trailers was impressive. The line-up of Chevy, Ford and Dodge trucks, both gas and diesel engines, with extended cabs, full to capacity represented a huge amount of horsepower to haul the load they needed.

The loaded trucks pulled their trailers to the fenced parking lot at the top of the ranch for the night. Trucks were detached from the trailers so owners could drive them home. At 3:00 a.m. the next morning they would arrive to hitch back up, load the horses and be on the road to begin the long haul to Albuquerque, New Mexico at 4:00 a.m.

Aunt Ginny and Uncle Mike hosted a wonderful outdoor barbeque for everyone with Aunt Ginny's famous tri-tips and steaks. The other women all brought dishes to share pot-luck style. Everyone ate until they were ready to burst. The party broke up early because the drive out time in the morning was set so they could get through the worst of the desert heat as early as possible for the horses.

Maryann had another reason to be looking forward to this trip. She'd been down the hill a few times and gone with Ginny and La Duquesa to Becky's home in San Juan Capistrano but she'd never been more than a hundred miles from home in her life. She'd never been out of the State of California. She'd looked up Arizona on her computer and found cactus that only grew there. She found pictures of New Mexico and Albuquerque to see what they looked like in pictures. She couldn't wait to see them for herself in person. This was a road-trip she looked forward to and she was bringing her best friend, La Duquesa, with her.

CHAPTER TWENTY-SIX

Hauling day began in pitch dark. People started arriving at Hartley Ranch in cars and trucks before 3 a.m. No one wanted to be late because the drive would be a long one. Horse trailers were hitched and moved back to the barn area so horses could be loaded. As soon as the last horse was in and secured, the trucks and other vehicles formed a line and headed out the gate to the freeway north bound for Arizona.

Becky and her parents left an hour and a half earlier than everyone else because they had an extra hundred miles to travel just to meet up with the caravan. They met the others at a stop just off the freeway in Barstow and continued on Highway 40 toward Needles, the Colorado River and Kingman, Arizona. They drove in darkness for the first hour and a half before the sun rose over the horizon. Dawn broke and Maryann didn't see much out the window driving toward Needles, California where they would cross the Colorado River into Arizona. The landscape was not much to look at on the stretch of road between Barstow and Needles. Rocks, low rocky hills, a few desert plants were about all she could see. There were few places to turn off the highway. Maryann and Brody laughed trying to pronounce the name Zzyzx, a health spa created by a quack doctor/preacher in the 1940's. Ginny finally told them it rhymed with "Isaac's."

After miles of driving through barren desert, Maryann was surprised at how green the edges of the Colorado River were as they approached the crossing into Arizona. The caravan stopped at the border to show the paperwork on the horses and get clearance from border patrol. That was their only stop until they reached Kingman. They pulled into a large truck-stop for fuel and to check on the horses. They refilled hay nets and offered water, got something to eat for themselves and got back on the road. With the sun up, the desert heated up too. They stopped again near Flagstaff, Arizona to check on the horses and offer them water laced with electrolytes. Flagstaff was near seven thousand feet in elevation so things cooled off a bit there. They picked up some lunch and snacks and continued east on Highway 40. They made a short fuel and horse watering stop at Holbrook, Arizona and didn't stop again until they reached Gallup, New Mexico.

At Gallup, everyone needed to get out of their vehicles to stretch their legs. They were still a ways from Albuquerque but wanted a short break. They checked the horses, refilled hay nets and brought them fresh buckets of water. Ginny added electrolytes to the water so the horses wouldn't dehydrate from the summer heat. The whole troop trudged into the restaurant at the truck stop for dinner and a bit of quick souvenir shopping before piling back in the vehicles and heading toward Grants, New Mexico. That would be their final stop before reaching Albuquerque.

Ginny pointed out where they crossed over the Continental Divide outside of Gallup. She explained to Maryann and Brody that is where the rivers change direction. On the west side, rivers run to the south and west but on the east side, they run south and east.

Maryann and Brody shared a map, marking places of interest off they would love to visit sometime. Maryann thought the Petrified Forest would be interesting, and some of the old Indian ruins too. Brody wanted to visit Monument Valley so he could put a foot and hand in four different states at the same time. He wanted to see the backdrop for so many old Western movies. They both wanted to see the caves at Carlsbad, New Mexico and the Plaza in Santa Fe.

It was near 6:00 p.m. when the caravan made their last stop at Grants for fuel. They checked the horses one more time and got back on the road within a few minutes. Ginny wanted to reach the fairgrounds in Albuquerque before nightfall if possible.

Ginny led the caravan onto the grounds of the New Mexico State Fairgrounds at 8:40 p.m. that evening. It was almost dark when the trucks pulled up to the barns they were assigned. The heavy work began as the girls bedded down the stalls and unloaded the horses. They hung buckets of water with electrolytes in each stall and hung freshly filled hay nets up for the horses.

Ginny directed people putting away tack, feed, show clothes, and other supplies in the ready-rooms and tack-rooms. Fathers and older boys stacked hay at the end of their barn. Mothers and daughters worked to organize everything as it came out of the vehicles and Ginny pointed directions for where to put things. They built portable closets to keep show clothes clean and dust free. Racks were mounted in the ready rooms for grooming supplies. Trunks containing coolers and blankets were stacked against the walls and indoor-outdoor carpets were laid in tack and ready-rooms to cover dirt floors. Men took ladders off the trucks and hung the stall drapes on the sides of the barns. Chris and Todd O'Neal and Charlie Reeves were already there and pitched in to help. As soon as the trucks were unloaded, they were moved to the trailer parking area to clear them out of the way.

Decorating began as soon as the gear was stowed and the stall drapes were tacked up. Chris's group got to see their posters for the first time. They were all excited with Maryann's art work. Stall signs went up. The glittery stars were mounted. The kids hung their posters next to each horse's stall. Todd and Charlie brought out their creations and Brody helped place the partial gazebo with benches next to the ready rooms adding lights along the top of the stalls and the roof of the gazebo. The plant guy delivered plants earlier that day so Chris and Ginny had them moved into position. Chris and Todd brought out their spot lights to light them from the bottom up along the stall walls. By 11:30 p.m. that night the work was finished. The adults thought the barn looked fabulous. Everyone sat down at tables and chairs and sipped soft drinks to relax for a few minutes. Folding director's chairs were Ginny's surprise for the kids. They had the kids' names painted on the back for them. That finished up the "Movie" theme and they were ready for the barn decorating competition which would take place the following day.

Several groups of other competitors came straggling by to see their decorations. They talked to each other and shared names, home locations, and information about activities taking place during the week-long competition. Some swapped phone numbers and contact information so they could keep in touch during and after the show. All the young people they met that night were just as excited about their horses and their accomplishments as the ones Chris O'Neal and Ginny brought with them. They encouraged one another.

The golf carts were delivered to the barn area and parked at the end nearest the arenas for later use. Everything was done! Everyone was dead on their feet. Grandpa and

Grandma Carnegie led the way to the hotel for the night. No one even thought about using the pool. All they wanted was a quick shower and to fall into bed. Tomorrow promised to be a busy day!

CHAPTER TWENTY-SEVEN

The horses settled in for the night. They ate some, drank some and napped standing up until the people left for the hotel for the night. Some chatted with each other, the ones from Ginny's barn getting to know the ones from Chris O'Neal's barn. They talked quietly so they didn't disturb other horses in the barns next to them.

Heidi's horse, Schultzy, tried and tried to reach out of his door and take a bite out of the rented plant alongside the barn front but couldn't quite reach it. He grumbled about that.

La Duquesa finally spoke up, "*Schultzy, leave that stuff alone. Those kids spent a lot of time making the barn look nice. Don't you dare mess it up for them.*"

Schultzy quipped back at her, "*And what are you going to do if I do, Little Miss Goody Two Shoes?*"

"*You could be messing with things you don't understand. Have you ever missed a meal before? Hasn't Heidi always fed you and kept you clean and exercised? I wouldn't goof that up if I were you. I've been starved and beaten. I know what it's like not having someone who loves you,*" she told him quietly.

Prince Ali stepped in. *"Yes, Schultzy, you need to mind your manners here. The kids have all worked hard to get us here. Let's not do anything to mess that up. I've missed a few meals myself, you know. You remember when I got to Ginny's ranch? Without my Becky, I went without food and water and was attacked by something like a barn cat on steroids. I would never do anything to hurt my Becky or even make her mad. I appreciate what our special people do for us. You should too."*

"Okay. Okay! You're right. I'll just get some sleep." Schultzy snapped and turned back inside his stall.

The other horses agreed with Prince Ali and La Duquesa. They appreciated their owners. They agreed they would not mess with the barn decorations. The barn settled into peace and quiet as the horses slept.

The competitors, along with Ginny, Brody and Chris, arrived early the next morning to feed and water their horses. None of them had a class until the next day so they were free to work with their horses individually and work with their coaches. Ginny and Chris set a time for the group to get their horses out for Showmanship practice.

The Region One youth representatives came to their barn early with the Region One Youth Advisor. They took one look at the barn decorations and asked Maryann if she would help them get ready for the Parade of Regions that night during Opening Ceremonies in Tingley Coliseum. She was flattered and immediately agreed to help. Each Region had a golf cart to decorate for the parade. The Region One kids had blank panels prepared to mount on their golf cart. Their plan was to cut photos out and paste them on the panels. When they saw the "movie" posters Maryann painted, they fell in love with her art work and wanted her to paint their panels instead. Grandpa drove them to the Region One area so Maryann could see the size of the panels and begin sketching drawings on them. The Region One Youth advisor promised to get the supplies she needed and be back within the hour.

Maryann quickly sketched horses on the panels. She used Prince Ali, the most famous horse on the show grounds, on the front panel in his Arabian native costume with palm trees and camels in the background. For the bay horse, she used Desperado in his western gear with the long horn cattle. She drew Schultzy, Heidi's chestnut hunter, with fox hounds. She sketched a lovely black Arabian English horse with a rider in a red day-coat in a park setting. By the time she finished her sketches, the Youth Advisor returned with her supplies and she got straight to work on the paintings. She finished by early afternoon so the kids could attach the paintings and finish decorating the golf cart before the parade.

Maryann hurried back to the barn so she could practice Showmanship with the others. The pattern was new and they all had to memorize it. After the judge looked at each horse in the line-up, they were to walk five paces forward, turn right and trot to the cone 25 feet away and halt. Then they were to half-turn to the rail and trot halfway around the arena, return to the line-up and halt again. It was an easy pattern, but easy to get confused if one were nervous. Each of the competitors practiced showing their horse to Chris and Ginny, making mental notes of their critique and practicing the pattern in a small arena off the beaten path from the other warm-up arenas that were so busy now.

When they finished the Showmanship coaching, everyone returned to the barn to get in some riding practice. Their horses needed to stretch their legs after the long ride the day before. Maryann had no chance to see other barns because she had been so occupied that day. She decided to walk La Duquesa past a couple on their way to a warm-up arena. She thought their barn looked better than most. She was happy she'd been able to help with that.

They reached the closest arena. It was full of other competitors working horses in every different discipline. She waited for an opening at the gate and pushed Quesa into a strong trot to enter as she'd been taught. They worked both directions in several gaits before Maryann looked for an opening at the gate to leave. She felt great. La Duquesa was perfect as usual. She had a good feeling about the competition. She returned to the barn and untacked Quesa, brushed her down and put her back in her stall with some goodies to munch on. She sat in her director's chair and relaxed.

Grandma Carnegie joined her. "You know your dad was an artist too, don't you?" she asked her.

"No! I didn't know that," Maryann admitted. "What did he do? Paint? Draw? Water Color?"

"Well, we're really going back a few years, my dear," Grandma Carnegie confessed. "I think the first thing he liked were pencil drawings. He was quite good, you know. Then he moved into pen and ink drawings. I think he did water colors after that and finally found oil painting was his passion. Your work reminds me of his sometimes. He was really good with light and shadow and texture. You could almost smell the apples in his still life paintings."

"Maybe that's where I get my talent from. Mom doesn't draw or paint. She's never done it that I know of. I don't mean she has no talent just I've never seen her do anything like drawing or painting," Maryann told her.

"Well, young lady, you come from a long line of talented women. There were a number of Carnegie women who showed a flair for the artistic. Some were wonderful designers of clothing. Some did design in their large outdoor gardens. Some did needle work and there were a few painters among them as I understand. I think that's where your father got his talent and probably you as well," she explained.

"Thank you, Grandma," Maryann said. "I'd like to learn more about my dad. I know more now than I did before. I also know he was a horseman and rode polo ponies. I bet he'd like La Duquesa too, wouldn't he?"

"He sure would, sweetheart," Grandma Carnegie hugged Maryann.

Ginny Hartley was getting anxious. There was no package waiting at the hotel front desk last night when she checked in. She hoped it would be there today. It was part of the deal between her and Charles Carnegie. Charles and Celeste did not want Maryann to know anything about them purchasing La Duquesa until the end of the competition in Albuquerque. They wanted it to be a surprise when they handed her La Duquesa's registration papers. Ginny called a friend of hers at the Arabian Horse Registry to find out how to accomplish that. She wanted the owner designation to be "Virginia Hartley" until the Carnegies were ready to make the announcement to Maryann. She had sent in copies of La Duquesa's registration papers with the entry forms for Youth Nationals but they would change the owner designation if the horse was re-registered before the competition.

Her friend suggested she send the paperwork to her attention at the Registry. She would make the change at the last minute and over-night the new registration papers to Ginny at the hotel before the competition. That way, should Maryann place in any of her classes, the announcer would call her number and name "La Duquesa, owned by Virginia Hartley and ridden by Maryann Wilcox" over the loudspeaker. Maryann wouldn't be the wiser.

Ginny checked her watch. It was 4:30 p.m. and almost everyone was at the barn. "Hey, guys, we probably need to make sure the horses are fed and get back to the hotel. We need to clean up for Opening Ceremonies," she announced. Everyone got up and began packing things away in the tack and ready rooms, feeding and watering horses, and picking up their personal belongings. Within a few minutes the last stragglers returned to the barn and got ready to leave.

Ginny had one more announcement to make. "I'd also like to tell you all that the Region One Director came to see me today. She and the Region One Youth Advisor asked Maryann Wilcox to ride their golf cart in the Parade of Regions with them and the Region One Youth of the Year! They think the Region One golf cart has a good shot at being the winner this year. They were pretty excited about Maryann's paintings."

Rose blushed with pride. She hadn't seen the paintings yet, but she watched her daughter painting the posters on the barn. She was so proud she could have burst her buttons. Adele and Roy joined her to congratulate Maryann along with Grandpa and Grandma Carnegie and the rest of the barn troop. La Duquesa nickered approval from her stall as well.

When Ginny checked in at the front desk of the hotel, there was a large envelope waiting for her. She breathed a sigh of relief and knocked on Charles and Celeste's hotel room door when she got to their floor. She handed Charles the envelope and quickly dashed off to her own room to get ready for the night's festivities.

Maryann showered, shampooed her hair, scrubbed her face until it glowed pink and brushed her teeth. She dried her hair and asked her mom for help getting it braided and into a pony tail before pulling on a clean sweater and clean pair of jeans. She took her barn boots outside on the veranda and scraped them as clean as she could. She dabbed a tiny bit of her mother's perfume behind her ears and stood up before her mother and slowly turned around so her mom could check her over. She passed inspection. Maryann had never met the Region One Director before and was a little nervous about riding in the parade with her. Her mom told her to "Sit back and enjoy it. You earned it!"

Rose drove Maryann to the fairgrounds with Roy and Adele. Grandpa and Grandma Carnegie followed them over. Most of their group was on the way. Maryann kissed her mom on the cheek and trotted to where the golf carts were getting ready for the parade. It was pandemonium there. The Region One cart was completely done but many of the others were getting their final touches and pulling into line in region order.

Hundreds of people were still filing into the Coliseum which held about seven thousand spectators. It was beautifully decorated with Regional logos, Sponsor logos, flowers and plants around the gazebo in the center of the arena and dangly strings of lights from the tall ceiling. The announcer and all those presented during the Opening Ceremonies were dressed in formal clothes, tuxedos for men and long sparkly gowns for the ladies.

The announcer addressed the crowd in Tingley Coliseum and welcomed them to the Youth National Championships. He introduced members of the Arabian Horse Association, Judges and Stewarts and staff members who would be there for the duration of the competition to help and assist parents and the young competitors. The final schedules for the competition were passed out in the stands and extras were left on tables at the exits.

When the announcer called for the Parade of Regions the cart Maryann rode in made a jerky start toward the arena floor. As they passed through the in-gate, the crowds began cheering and clapping. The Regional One Director drove the cart around the arena with the other eighteen Regions following behind them. The carts parked circling the arena. Judges walked the arena floor stopping by each Region's cart, making notes on their pad and walking to the next cart.

They grouped together in the gazebo and compared notes then handed the announcer a list.

As they waited for the judges' decision, the Region One Cart pulled to the gazebo in the center and the Region One Director brought a large basket of candy to a giant barrel at center ring and dumped it in. The announcer told the crowd the candy barrel was there for all the youngsters and it was part of the "All for the kids" atmosphere of the competition. Any kid who wanted candy was welcome to visit the Welcome Booth and help themselves. One by one the other Regions dumped their baskets in the barrel until it was completely full to the point of spilling over.

When all the carts were back in their place along the rail, the announcer called for Region One, Region Four, Region 11 and Region 19 to the center of the ring. The Judges handed out ribbons while the announcer called the winners, beginning with Region One as First Place in the competition!

Once the cheering from the golf cart competition died down the announcer called a few trainers into the center ring. Ginny Hartley and Chris O'Neal were among the names called. As soon as all the trainers stood in the center ring, the announcer told everyone they had winners for the Barn Decorating Competition to award. They would be handed to the trainers responsible for their barns. This time the announcer began with Fourth Place. The trainer received a trophy and ribbons for each of his competitors. Then Third Place was announced. It wasn't Ginny or Chris. The announcer called the next trainers for Second Place and it still wasn't Ginny or Chris. The members of their barn exploded with clapping and cheering. Ginny and Chris were called for First Place in the Barn Decorating Competition. The kids in their group met them at the in-gate hugging, yelling, and hollering. Maryann barely made it in time because she rode the winning cart back to the Region One booth for display during the competition.

The rest of the evening was a blur for Maryann. So many people sought her out to congratulate her on her artwork. Many of the other kids stopped to talk to her and get her contact information because they wanted her to do pictures of their horses. She didn't understand all the fuss. She did what she did because she loved doing it. Her real passion was La Duquesa but she loved to paint horses. She wondered what else would happen during the week.

CHAPTER TWENTY EIGHT

C harlie Spade called his friend Sam Brown. "Hey Sam, how about we have lunch at Denny's again. I've been thinking about the Reilly Stone case. Why don't you bring your Murder Book with you so we can go over the scene photos?"

Sam searched through records for a couple of months trying to piece together the life of an invisible man, as he thought of him. Reilly Stone had no direct means of support. He had no job but he could afford to pay cash for a new Mercedes every year. He couldn't locate a bank account. His Social Security account had been dormant since he was sixteen years old and worked as a burger flipper in New Jersey. There were no police records on file for the man in New Jersey or California or anywhere in between that he could find. Who was this guy? What was he doing at that cabin? Who killed him? He had a few vague suspicions but not one concrete fact to build a case on.

He was happy to meet Charlie for lunch. Sometimes they solved crimes together and sometimes not, but at least he'd have a decent lunch and a good cup of coffee!

Charlie and Sam met in the parking lot of their favorite Denny's and walked inside together. Charlie asked the hostess to seat them in a booth away from the crowd. He didn't think the murder scene photos would be a good appetizer for the general public.

While they waited for their order, they sipped coffee and caught up on the doings of their families and other mutual friends. Once the waitress put plates in front of them and walked away to wait on other tables, Charlie said, "What was your overall impression of Sara Evans now that you've had time to think about it?"

"Well, I'd say she was scared to death when I first met her," Sam said thoughtfully. "That fear seemed to center on Reilly Stone. Her demeanor changed quite a bit after I gave her the bad news."

"I got the impression she'd been looking over her shoulder when she first came to see me," Charlie remarked. "She was nervous about something but I chalked it up to sorrow over her aunt's death. She told me they were very close and her aunt passed away a few months after diagnosis. I do believe she was still in shock over it."

"Then there was the thing about her clothes," Sam remembered. "We talked about that the last time we got together. It was 80 degrees outside and she was wearing a long sleeved, turtle necked sweater. Who does that?"

"Yeah, and those bruises on her arm," Charles said. "The bruises she put off on dropping a box of her aunt's things. And how about the dark glasses? That was strange too, remember?"

"Yes, I do," Sam nodded. "There was definitely something more going on than she was telling us."

"Well, let's just suppose she was at the cabin the night Reilly Stone died. And let's suppose she was going there to check on the horse's welfare. And let's suppose the horse was missing. And let's suppose Reilly Stone was out shopping when she got there so she walked into the cabin alone. Didn't you tell me there was beer and whiskey in the trunk of his car when you arrived at the murder scene? Obviously he had not had time to unload his car. Then let's suppose our Sara walked into a mess in the cabin. Didn't you also tell me her house was neat as a pin? If she lived in the cabin for a couple of months with her aunt, I would assume she left it clean and tidy if that's her normal habit. I think you told me the place was a wreck when you got there and it didn't appear to be vandals."

Sam pondered for a minute then said, "Yes, and to complete the thoughts, let's suppose Reilly Stone came in and surprised Sara. I know she looks a little timid on the outside, but I know how my wife can turn into a bear if I leave a mess in her kitchen!" he laughed. "And from what I could see, that place was really trashed. But, I didn't go inside because it looked like an accidental death and everything was on the outside of the cabin, not inside it."

"Got it," Charlie said. "Then, let's suppose she yelled at him for making a mess. We already know he was drunk. So maybe he attacked her. That would account for the bruises on her arm, the possible black eye and maybe bruises on her neck that caused her to wear a turtleneck sweater and dark glasses to hide it."

"Yeah, but the Coroner said Reilly Stone was six foot, three inches tall and 225 pounds. If I were a betting man, I'd say Sara Evans is five feet, two inches tall and maybe 115 pounds soaking wet. If Reilly Stone had her around the throat, what chance would she have?"

"Absolutely none!" Charlie agreed. "But what if she found something within reach that she could swing and hit him with, like maybe a heavy flat object like the coroner thought? Didn't you say the coroner felt it was a heavy, flat object?"

"Let's take a look at the photos. Maybe something will jump out at us," Sam suggested.

He opened the book and paged through all the documents until he got to the photos. The waitress came to top off their cups and he quickly shut the book while she was at the table. The photos were a bit gruesome. As soon as she left, he pulled it open again and paged through the photos until he came to the ones the photographer shot from the outside of the cabin in through the front door.

"There!" Charlie said excitedly. "Would you look at that?" his finger pointed at a dark shape lying under the end table across from the front door.

Sam stared at it. "Well, I'll be darned. If that doesn't look like a cast iron skillet, I don't know what does!"

Charlie spun the book around and pulled it closer so he could have a better look. "Didn't you tell me the coroner found bacon grease in his hair and on his clothes? Well, I think we just found our murder weapon and there's a streak of something that looks like grease around it too."

"My guess is he was trying to choke her and she grabbed whatever she could lay a hand on. If she took a swing at him with that skillet, it would be a blow with a heavy flat object. Maybe we found the remains of his last meal all over him too," Sam suggested.

"What do we do with this?" Charlie asked.

"I know Sara was scared out of her mind when I stopped by to see her a week or so after Stone's death. I think she was scared of Reilly Stone. She had no idea he was dead. She'd probably been locked up in that house afraid he would show up there at any time. And there's the bruising that she tried to hide. I'd bet you anything she had no idea she killed him."

"What do you think the District Attorney is going to say about it?" Charlie asked.

"I don't think this is even going to the District Attorney. I'll talk to my boss. Even if Sara knew he was dead, it looks to me like a case of self-defense, not murder. Don't you agree?"

"That's where I'd place my bet." Charlie said. He closed the Murder Book and slid it back across the table.

"By the way, I did find that horse for Sara," Charlie told Sam. "I went through the Arabian Horse Registry and found the horse was re-registered to a Virginia Hartley in Pinon Hills so I went to see her. She only lives a few miles from the cabin where Stone died. She showed me photos of the horse she and her husband "rescued" from Reilly Stone. She was in bad shape! Mrs. Hartley also showed me a young girl at her ranch riding that horse while I was there. Sure was a different animal, and she looked happy."

"Sounds like you earned your exorbitant fee this time," Sam chuckled

"Yup, sure did. And the best part is the young lady's grandparents bought the horse for her. Paid Sara twenty five thousand dollars for her," Charlie laughed. "That's more than I paid for my wife's car."

The two men had a good laugh. They also had a good laugh remembering how their former coworkers thought they should swap first names. They finished their lunch and promised to get together again soon.

CHAPTER TWENTY NINE

L a Duquesa was caught up in the excitement of the Youth Championship show. She wanted to do well for Maryann. She concentrated hard when Maryann rode her in the warmups and when they practiced Showmanship. She remembered being at the National Championship with Anne Stone and Tania last year. She concentrated hard then too and Anne was so proud of her. She knew Anne was happy and so was Tania. She wanted to make Maryann feel the same way.

After the Opening Ceremonies, the troop from Chris and Ginny's barn made the rounds of other barns to see their displays. The food vendors were in high gear putting out food from every culture and lots of it. Giant tents were set up with displays of everything for sale from horse tack to clothing, sculptures to photography to paintings of Arabian Horses. Top Ten Jackets were already available. If you made a Top Ten placing you could buy one and have your name embroidered on it with the date. National Champion Jackets hung right beside them waiting for the winners. Maryann spent time touring the facilities with her Mom, Aunt and

Uncle and Grandpa and Grandma. Grandpa promised her one of the jackets if she placed high enough to earn it. She was excited. Rose did a little shopping early for Christmas when she could sneak off for a few minutes. Grandma told Maryann to pick out a piece of art that she liked as a souvenir. Maryann chose a small bronze horse that looked a lot like La Duquesa. She wanted to put it on her dresser so she would always have a reminder of her best friend looking at her before she went to sleep at night.

People began drifting away from the fairgrounds early that night. There were classes beginning at 8:00 in the morning. By 11:00 that night, the fairgrounds were nearly deserted except for the horses.

Prince Ali was stabled next to La Duquesa. She saw him regularly when Ginny took her and Maryann to San Juan Capistrano to practice with him and Becky. She liked him. He had a kind nature and was always the gentleman even though his handsome looks make her heart pitter-patter from time to time. He was nice to talk to. And they shared something else in common. Each of them would be riding in this show with their best friends.

"What's it like for you when Becky rides you?" she asked him.

"It's the most wonderful thing in the world!" Ali told her. *"Becky is my best friend. I would climb mountains and fight off monsters to be with her. She ticks to my tock. When we go riding, sometimes I get feelings like I know what she wants me to do before she asks me and I go ahead and do it and it's always right. I've never had that happen with anyone else, just Becky. I know when she's happy and I know when she's sad. She tells me a lot of things she doesn't tell her Mom. Is that strange?"*

"I don't know if it's strange. I sort of get a feeling like that with Maryann, but maybe more than just a feeling. When she rides me it's like she becomes a part of me, like another leg or something. We move together like we are one and not two beings,

even if we are so different. It is the most enjoyable thing for me. I haven't had that many people ride on my back so I thought I'd ask you about it," Quesa said quietly.

"Well, Pretty Lady, I'm guessing Maryann is your one special *human. I got lucky to be born into the family with mine. You have found yours so you are very lucky too,"* he told her.

"What does it mean, your one special human, anyway? I *thought I'd found mine with my last owner but she died and my circumstances changed terribly. The day Maryann came into my stall and scrunched down under the feeder and read a book to me I knew. But it felt like I'd always known her somehow and I'd just met her. Does that make any sense to you?"* she asked.

Ali yawned and stretched his neck. *"It does. We depend on humans. Some of us get lucky and have humans that also depend on us. I think humans are complicated. And I think there are good humans and bad humans. You are I are fortunate to be living with really good humans. Relax and enjoy it. Things happen. Treasure what you have now so you have it to remember if things change for you again. Remembering my Becky got me through some pretty tough times."* he told her. *"We probably should get some rest now. I think tomorrow's going to be a big day for us. Good luck with your classes. I know you will do well."*

"You have a good night's sleep too. I hope you and Becky knock the socks off your competitors. Thanks for sharing with me. Good night," Quesa told him before she walked to the back of her stall and dropped down in the straw for a few minutes. It felt good to take her weight off her feet for a while. La Duquesa dozed off.

The barn troop arrived at the fairgrounds at 5:30 a.m.with their adrenalin pumping. Today had a busy schedule with preliminary classes for half of the young people. They needed to place in the top ten in the preliminaries to qualify for the semi-final classes. They had to place in the top ten in the semi-finals to qualify for the finals where the National

Champions would be awarded. All the horses had to be fed and the ones showing that day had to be bathed so they could be groomed to show. Brody and the youngsters not showing helped the ones that were. Chris and Ginny directed traffic. Ginny had the master schedule in the Ready Room for everyone to check. Different arenas were being used for different disciplines and there were horses to show in every one of them. Ginny and Chris both thanked Charles Carnegie silently again for the thoughtful renting of the golf carts.

Parents and other relatives arrived before 8:00 a.m. to check the schedule and get to the correct arena to watch their youngsters. Food Vendors were in full swing again pumping out everything from tacos and hot dogs on a stick to smoked turkey legs and pancakes with sausages. Every barn was bustling. Vendors in the tents manned their booths. Everywhere you looked was colorful with signs advertising food for sale, bright riding outfits, silver trim on saddles and horses that gleamed in the early morning sunlight.

Chris O'Neal's son, Todd, had a preliminary round in the outside arena for the Reining class on Desperado and easily placed in the top ten. Ginny's student, Heidi, had a preliminary round for flat Hunters-Under-Saddle Ages 14 to 18 with Schultzy and also placed in the top ten. Susie and Dreamer competed in the Hunters-Under-Saddle Ages 13 and Under and made the cut. There was barely enough time to get from the arena where Todd was showing to the arena where Heidi and Susie were. With the help of the golf carts and a few round trips, all the families and the other competitors from the barn got to watch all three in their classes before lunchtime that day. The entire group returned to the barn for lunch bringing food of every kind in from the Food Vendors. The whole barn was excited. It had been a very good morning with three classes down and three of their pairs moving on to the semi-finals later in the week. The only pair left to show that day was Maryann and La Duquesa.

After she finished eating, Maryann haltered La Duquesa and took her for a walk around the barn area to relax a little before getting ready for their class. She just wanted to spend some time with her best friend alone. She talked to Quesa and told her about her hopes they wouldn't break the winning streak set that morning. Quesa understood every word and had the same hopes. She didn't want to let Maryann down. She thought to herself, *I will do my very best for you because I love you.*

When Maryann and La Duquesa returned to the barn to get ready, Becky, Brody and Todd were the only ones there. Everyone else wondered off to watch other classes. Maryann was actually glad. She'd met Todd over the phone with Becky but got to know him better when they met the day they arrived. He, Brody and Becky were her favorites. She was secretly glad they would be the ones to help her with Quesa.

Ginny returned to the barn just as Maryann was mounting Quesa to warm her up. Ginny inspected the pair and nodded her head to acknowledge they were ready for competition. "Let's go watch this pretty girl dance for you, shall we?" she said to Maryann. Brody, Todd and Becky came along with Ginny and Maryann to the warm up arena. Maryann watched for an opening and cued La Duquesa to her strong trot to enter. She had several passes in both directions and at different gaits before exiting.

"She feels fantastic today!" Maryann said with enthusiasm. "She's moving perfectly and I think she likes this," Maryann stroked Quesa's neck gently. "don't you girl?" La Duquesa nodded her head as if in agreement. Becky giggled.

"Ali does that too sometimes when I talk to him. It looks like she's agreeing with you!" she told Maryann.

Maryann's class was the last preliminary round for the day. Everyone from their barn was in the stands watching as Maryann and La Duquesa danced into the arena at her strong trot. It was breathtaking to watch. Scores of people in the stands singled them out to observe as they changed gaits and directions at the call of the announcer, never missing a stride, always in perfect unison. It was no surprise to anyone there that Maryann and La Duquesa were placed first on all three judges' cards making them eligible for the semi-finals too.

The only problem that came up at the barn was Prince Ali. He wasn't the problem but his fans were as soon as word passed around that he was there to show. People saw his pictures in the newspapers and on TV after he was drugged and stolen from the Swallows Day Parade in San Juan Capistrano earlier that year. Becky was hurt trying to defend him. Her picture was in the papers and on TV with him. Fans stopped Walter and Caroline Howard and Becky everywhere they went to talk about their famous horse. The barn was mobbed with fans who wanted to see him in person. The adults got together to discuss the problem. His fans were curious about him, but the numbers of them stopping by created problems for everyone at the barn. It was almost impossible to get him out of his stall by the end of the first day of competition and the crowding also created problems for the other competitors trying to get their horses out and ready.

Charles Carnegie came up with a solution. He called the fairgrounds office and got a phone number. He called and paid for private security staff to help maintain order at the barn and to watch over the horses through the night so the Howards and Prince Ali could get some sleep. After what happened in San Juan Capistrano, they feared leaving him alone and unguarded once the word about his presence spread and the fans showed up in large numbers.

Walter Howard talked to Charles about the bill for private security and wanted to pay it himself. Charles laughed, "Walter, your daughter has been so kind to my beautiful granddaughter please let me do this for you. I really mean it. I want to take care of it for you as my small way of thanking you and your wife and daughter for your kindness."

From that moment two security officers accompanied Prince Ali whenever he left the stall. They cordoned off the area so they could let fans see Ali one or two at a time when it was convenient for the Howards. The officers came wearing bullet proof vests under military style uniforms that looked like they meant business. Whenever Ali was out of his stall, at least one other security officer monitored the barn.

The hub bub simmered down gradually. The Howards were able to breathe again without fear. But Becky was anxious anyway. She and Maryann talked about it when they had some privacy. "Ali is used to winning all the time. Everyone here expects him to win. What if I flub up a class and don't make the cut?" she asked Maryann. Her first preliminary round was fast approaching.

"You and Ali are a team! All you have to do is relax. He's a winner and so are you! Just go out there and ride him like you do at home. You'll be great. Stop worrying. Relax and breathe," Maryann told her. "I was afraid before our first class too, but I took ten deep breaths just before I cued her to trot into the arena. As soon as we got through the in-gate, I rode her like we do at home. You can do it too! I know you can!"

Becky giggled. "You sound just like me. That's the same advice I gave you before your preliminary isn't it? You're saying I should take my own advice?"

"Yeah, buddy! Get out there and have some fun!" Maryann giggled back.

As expected, Becky and Prince Ali had a perfect ride. They made the cut unanimously. They were in the semi-finals.

The only class the competitors were entered in where they had to compete with each other directly was the Showmanship class. There were eight of them from Chris and Ginny's barn. If they worked hard, maybe they could sweep the class to make the finals. That would leave two places left. Could they do it?

CHAPTER THIRTY

As hoped for, by the end of the second day of competition all eight of the young people from Chris and Ginny's barn made the cut in their preliminary rounds so they would be in the semi-finals for their divisions and classes. Over the next three days most of them were scheduled to compete in their semi-final rounds. Anxiety ramped up as the classes got nearer. Because they would be competing against each other in the Showmanship class, Chris and Ginny got their group together at the far end of the fairgrounds as often as they could to drill and practice.

When the Showmanship class was called, all eight of the youngsters and their horses trotted through the in-gate and around the arena to their places in the line-up and waited their turn in front of the judges. Each of them remembered the pattern and performed it flawlessly.

The wait while the judges turned in their notes at the center ring and tallies were done seemed endless for the competitors. Chris and Ginny stayed at the rail and requested their kids maintain their posture while they waited for the decision. Some of the other kids relaxed along the rail and talked to their friends, trainers and parents.

At last the announcer called the class to order to make the presentations. He began by announcing 10th place. When it was over and placings were called, all eight of Chris and Ginny's kids made the top ten. Becky and Prince Ali won the Championship! Maryann and La Duquesa were awarded the Reserve Championship! Todd O'Neal and Desperado took third place! Other barns took sixth and tenth places. The kids, parents, other family members and fans of Prince Ali cheered until they were hoarse. The security guards had a more difficult time walking back to the barn with Prince Ali this time. Fans everywhere wanted to have their pictures taken with him, wanted to pet him and talk to the Howards about him.

The Championship trophies were beautiful statues of Arabian horses in Gold, Silver and Bronze mounted on walnut bases. These three were the first to be displayed on a special table set up for them at the barn. The Top Ten ribbons and Championship/Reserve Championship Rose garlands were hung on the end of the barn as part of their display.

As the week progressed, most of the kids made their semi-final cuts in all divisions. Championship classes were held at the end of the week. Todd O'Neal added a Gold Championship trophy to the table for Reining with Desperado, then added another one for Western Pleasure Ages 14 to 18. In a surprise to his dad, he added one more for Western Dressage. Todd and Desperado were the team to beat in the Western Division for kids 14 to 18 years of age. Charlie Reeves, from Chris's stable, added his own trophies in the Western Division for kids 13 and under with his horse Ace High.

Melissa's horse, Mighty Max, was a surprise at the show. They placed right behind Todd in Showmanship then went on to win the National Championship in Half-Arabian English Pleasure for Ages 13 and Under. He was a tough competitor. He was over 16 hands tall with the loud coloring of a bay and white Pinto. His neck was long, his topline level, shoulders well laid back and he had four perfectly straight legs. He had the lovely face of his mother with large eyes set wide, nice jibah, or dish, and small muzzle typical of an Arabian. Melissa entered him in the Halter in Hand class. The Halter Finals were all held on the final night of the show in Tingley Coliseum where other very popular class finals were held.

When Melissa, who was running as fast as she could, came flying into the arena with Mighty Max on the lead, his ground pounding stride felt like it tripped the Richter Scale at 5.5!

He was an instant hit with the nearly seven thousand spectators. He stood for the judge like a pro. When the class was called and Mighty Max won the Championship, Melissa dropped to her knees in surprise, then jumped up on his back and threw her arms around his neck hugging him for dear life. She slid off to accept the award and let the judge place the red roses around his neck, then took off with him running his victory lap around the coliseum to screaming fans.

Finals night also included the Championship Classes for Purebred Native Costume for Ages 13 and Under, Country English Pleasure for Ages 13 and Under and the English Pleasure Class for Ages 13 and Under. Becky had two different costumes to wear with Prince Ali. Fortunately the classes were separated far enough during the evening session for her to get back to the barn and change between them.

Native Costume came first. Becky and Ali wore the same teal velvet and Swarovski crystal costume he'd worn during the parade in San Juan Capistrano before their tragedy. This time, however, Ali was not being asked to walk the street, he was asked to fly. He entered the arena at a hand gallop that covered twenty-five feet per stride, much like the ground eating stride of a thoroughbred race horse at full gallop. Ali, however, lifted his knees above level with the ground and curled his hooves under himself while his back feet launched him into the air so that he appeared to float. His fans screamed with excitement. The dangly lights from the arena ceiling and the other arena lighting sparkled off the crystals on his costume so they appeared to burn like fire with every movement. It was dazzling! Becky was exhilarated. It was the most exciting ride she'd had with Ali. She hung on and went with it. Half way through the class everyone in the Coliseum knew who the winner was.

Prince Ali and Becky brought home another Championship trophy for Mom's trophy cases and they weren't done yet.

While Becky was riding in the Native Costume Class, Maryann was getting La Duquesa ready for her final class of the show. Her mom, Brody and Chris O'Neal rushed back to the barn to help her get ready while the others stayed at the coliseum to watch Becky and Ali. Chris and Brody walked with her to the warm up ring and watched her enter at a strong trot. She made several passes and exited, ready for her last class. Chris and Brody escorted Maryann and Rose back to the coliseum, quietly offering Maryann a few words of encouragement to help her and La Duquesa with their competition.

Just as Maryann and La Duquesa arrived near the in-gate waiting area, the crowd exploded inside Tingley Coliseum as Becky and Ali made their Victory pass. Ginny came dashing out to see Maryann before her class was called. Maryann was strangely quiet and sedate as she sat on Quesa's back. Quesa was the same. Ginny saw something unusual happen right in front of her. La Duquesa's name in English was The Duchess and the mare took on the air of Royalty. Maryann matched it. When the in-gate for their class opened, the pair entered the arena with the attitude they owned it. La Duquesa was a noble creature, both beautiful and proud. The pair danced on air with elegance and grace. The spectators went wild again! As with Becky and Ali, the class was over before it was called. None of the other horses came close to them in any way. Maryann cried when La Duquesa's name was announced as Champion. She was immensely proud of her and proud of herself. They did it! They did it together! Maryann came from poverty. La Duquesa came from starvation, brutality and neglect. They were champions together! Nothing in this world or the next would ever feel so good to Maryann as the exhilaration she felt at that moment and she shared it with her best friend!

Maryann realized she just had time to get Quesa back to the barn and taken care of before Becky's last class of the show. She'd missed the Native Costume class but she didn't want to miss the English Pleasure class. She and Brody quickly walked Quesa back to the barn, removed her tack, checked her water and gave her the goodies she'd been holding for her. She hugged Quesa an extra time or two before they dashed back to the Coliseum just in time to see Becky and Ali enter the arena.

Prince Ali was every inch a champion from his first hoof print in the arena to his last. His high floating trot was different from Quesa's but every bit as elegant in its own way. Ali and Becky easily won their last class and added one more Gold trophy to the stack on the display table at the barn. The ribbons and rose garlands covered the end of the barn and spread around the sides as well after Becky's last ride of the show.

The troop followed Becky and Ali with their security guards back to the barn that night high on life. They learned so much from the competition in New Mexico. They learned how to be a good winner and not take their successes too seriously. They learned how to be good sportsmen and women by sharing with others and not bashing them. They cheered each other on as strongly as the others cheered them on when their turn in the arena came. They found substitutes for broken tack and torn clothes to help other competitors. They shared tips they heard from someone else more knowledgeable. They shared names and contacts from around the country among themselves and with those from other barns. Some, like Todd O'Neal, decided to get involved with the Arabian Youth Council. Some decided to get involved in Youth Judging so they could view riders as the judges saw them. They all grew as people and as horsemen and horsewomen. Ginny and Chris were so proud of their group of kids.

As soon as Prince Ali was untacked and returned to his stall, Ginny called the group together for a few minutes.

"I have something to say to all of you," she began. "I've never seen a trophy table more full in my life, even when I was competing like you did this week. I love each and every one of you for being consistent, hardworking, and talented, but I also love the fact that you've supported each other and many other competitors this week from other places in our country. I'd like to say one thing – Good Job! Every one of you did the best you were capable of. That goes for each of you, Todd, Melissa, Heidi, Kathy, Susie, Becky, Maryann, Charlie and Brody," she looked at each of them in turn. "I could not be more proud of you."

Grandpa Carnegie stepped up in front of the group. Ginny quietly slipped behind everyone and haltered La Duquesa in her stall, slipping her stall door open.

"I have something to say here as well. Mrs. Carnegie and I have thoroughly enjoyed our week with you young people and your families. We did notice something this week. We noticed that six of you youngsters owned your own horses. There were only two competitors here that were showing someone else's horse and we're going to fix one of them right now. Maryann, could you step over here?" Grandma Carnegie slipped him a large piece of paper. "I have something here for you," Grandpa Carnegie said to her as he handed the paper to her.

While everyone was distracted with the suspense, Ginny quietly walked La Duquesa around the group and came up behind Grandma and Grandpa Carnegie.

Maryann stared at the paper in her hand. Her hand began to shake. It was La Duquesa's registration papers. The name of the owner was ... did she misread that? No, she didn't. The owner listed on the papers was Maryann Wilcox and it had her address on it! Tears filled her eyes as she stared at the names on the piece of paper once again to be sure.

"Why don't you say hello to your horse, Maryann?" Ginny said quietly as she handed Maryann the lead rope.

Maryann didn't know what to do first. Hug her horse? Hug her grandparents? Hug Ginny? Hug her mother? Or just cry for happy. So she did a little of each and tried not to drop the paper that meant so much to her and her best friend.